1

Wish You Were Here

Annette Scannell

4

Wish You Were Here

Annette Scannell

Chapter One

Before I turned thirteen years old, I knew my mother wouldn't be coming back. I can't remember the exact moment I realised, but it wasn't long after we returned home from holiday in August 1976. It was the hottest summer since records began or in living memory, or something like that. My mother was blonde and fair-skinned and not built for that kind of heat. When it became clear we were heading for a heatwave, she set up the sewing machine in the dining room and spent the whole of July running up a variety of cotton dresses for herself. Her favourite fabrics were covered in tiny floral prints, often orange or a mixture of oranges, pinks and yellows. And I would have wide elasticated hairbands, Jackie-O style, fashioned from the off-cuts. Mum had a scent, sweet and flowery, which matched the dresses. She was floral and fragrant and willowy, a cottage garden come to life.

Every year, we spent our holidays in the same north-eastern beauty spot. 'Here, we have the countryside *and* the seaside,' my father observed with satisfaction on more than one occasion. We stayed at the same farm nestled in the Northumbrian countryside just a short drive from the sea. The best of both worlds, according to Dad, as if this windswept, godforsaken place was the most sought-after holiday destination on earth. And we children knew no better.

But the summer of '76 was the exception. There was no wind, no rain, only incessant sunshine nationwide, baking the pavements and gardens from coast to coast. The car was packed to the hilt with suitcases and bags of all sizes. My mother brought enough provisions to last at least for the first week. 'They don't have Leo's up there; I can't understand it,' she told us with a note of disappointment. No other supermarket would do. My sister and I were packed too, squashed tightly on the back seat of the blue Cortina with our vanity cases and a large cool box wedged between us. In the days before compulsory seatbelts, this was probably the safest way to travel. The drive took a sweaty and irritable five hours up the motorway. Even with all four windows wound right down and a tropical gale blowing through the car, the heat was unbearable. We played long, tedious games of *I Spy*. But there is only so much to spy along the M6: other vehicles, specific parts of other vehicles, fields, sheep, bridges, trees, that's about it. And when our minds were sufficiently numbed, we would nod off to sleep, except Dad of course, who was driving.

In 1976 my world was a heady mix of Enid Blyton, horses, and Jackie magazine. I was caught between childhood and adolescence, in an idyll of secret islands, Black Beauty and burgeoning hormones. My sister, four years younger than me, was not yet aware of much more in life than her Sindy doll and enchanted woods. She and I usually spent a good deal of our holidays wandering around the farmyard and barns taking in the sweet smell of hay and pigs and chasing the occasional chicken. We longed for adventure, for mystery and for the unexpected to happen. But it never did. Until 1976.

Turning into the drive at Newell farm was, to us, the most exciting thing in the world. We were escaping from the city and school and the excitement never waned, despite every holiday being a replica of the previous year. On the opposite side of the road from the main part of the farm, there were more cottages owned by the Newell family. They were set in a terrace, and I was glad we didn't have to stay there with close neighbours to cramp our style. Our little cottage sat just inside the drive, detached with its own small front garden and a field behind.

'Go and unpack your things,' Mum told us as she emptied the food bags into the larder of the tiny kitchen. And she stopped for a moment by the sink, to gaze through the window at two horses grazing in the field. The air outside was still and silent but for the horses tearing the grass and a pheasant calling in a far-off copse of trees. No breeze, just the gently cooling evening filled with the aromatic scent of honeysuckle and manure.

On the first morning of our holiday, I felt that delicious sense of anticipation and excitement at waking up in a different place than usual. I lay for a while on the lumpy mattress, arms behind my head, enjoying the holiday feeling. My sister and I shared the bedroom which smelt of mothballs and *Lily of the Valley* perfume. The remnants of all past visitors seemed to linger in the room, imprinted, like ghosts, into the walls, the air and the candlewick bedspreads. I wondered what this year's holiday would bring. Visions of all the local attractions we would be going to crowded into my mind. But to be honest, I would have been happy just staying at the cottage, mooching about the farmyard all day, visiting the horses and acting out complex *Black Beauty*-style plotlines in my head.

Further up the drive from Groom's cottage stood the main house. Not your common-or-garden farmhouse, Newell Hall was more of a stately home. It had wide wrought iron gates, a cobbled forecourt and landscaped gardens. This was an upper-class, hunting, shooting and fishing kind of farm. Goodness knows where my parents found out about it. Or how they afforded it. The self-styled gentleman farmer, Mr. Newell strode down the drive each morning in his tweeds and *plus-fours*, born too late for the kind of life he really aspired to. We could hear him before we saw him, bellowing orders at the farm workers in his thinly disguised northern accent.

'God, he likes the sound of his own voice,' my father said one morning after being woken at seven-thirty. But at least our impromptu early morning alarm call meant we were up and ready to make the most of the day by nine o' clock. And today was going to be a long day of holiday fun starting with a trip to the seaside town of Seahouses.

Because it was so early, the shops and cafés were only just opening and setting up when we arrived. There was much clattering of chairs and shutters and a lot of cheerful shopkeepers greeting each other, anticipating a hopefully lucrative day of tourist trade. We had some breakfast at a greasy spoon café and then wandered round the streets for a while, looking at the cheap souvenir shops. My sister bought a small plastic grey seal with her pocket money. The whole town smelt of fish and chips and candy floss. From the seafront we strained our eyes to see the Faroe isles swathed in mist, too far away to identify the seals and puffins that gather there. Mum suggested a boat trip, but Dad rejected that idea, saying he didn't have the legs for it and that he'd seen his full English breakfast once today and didn't want to see it again.

By eleven, the sun had all but burned away the sea-fret that had been sitting stubbornly over land and water. And we realised another sweltering day was on the cards. We sat on the beach for a while, Dad in his smart trousers and open-necked polo shirt and Mum in her print dress and her usual vibrant red lipstick. We all took off our shoes to feel the warm, fine sand against our feet. My sister and I wished we had brought our swimming things from the cottage. We had left so early we hadn't thought properly about what we might need. But we had a paddle anyway in the sharpness of the North Sea shallows.

'I think we should pop back to the cottage, and I'll make a picnic. We can take it into the countryside,' Mum offered. Dad was in full agreement. That way we could appreciate our unique geographical position all in one day.

Whilst she put together egg and cress sandwiches, my sister and I visited the two horses in the field behind the cottage. I had no fear, even though one of the horses was an enormous shire. I was straight over the gate and into the field to stroke and pat them. Then I saw someone had got there before us.

'Hi there,' called the young woman waving and shielding her eyes from the sun. She was dressed in jodhpurs, short boots, a t-shirt and quilted gilet, her blonde hair pulled roughly into a ponytail. She was everything I wanted to be: pretty, suntanned, outdoorsy, with fabulously casual equine style. She beckoned us over, me and my sister, to where she was putting a bridle on Bay.

'Hi, are you staying at Groom's cottage?' she asked. I nodded, dumbstruck. She smiled. 'Are you enjoying your holiday?'

It was my sister's turn to nod. I patted Bay's smooth, copper coloured shoulder and found my voice. 'Yes, thanks. I love your horses.'

'Oh, do you? Can you ride?'

'Yes, I go riding once a fortnight.' This was not strictly true, I did go riding, but only when my parents could afford it. Even so, I could trot and even canter a bit. So once a fortnight sounded fair.

'Gosh, well perhaps you could ride Bay for me sometimes,' she paused, then added: 'If you'd like to, that is?'

If I'd like to? All my Christmases came at once on that glorious day. *What a thing.* I could pretend Bay was mine, my

12

own horse. To be able to go riding alone in the open countryside, it was a dream come true for me.

Carly Newell was probably about twenty years old in 1976. In the three summers we had stayed at Newell farm I had not met her before. Later I found out that she had been studying abroad during that time and her trips home had never coincided with our holidays. I still remember her standing in the sunny field that day, her bright smile and her blonde hair escaping from its ponytail. She was the epitome of fresh-faced, laid-back, country-girl style, and as a horse loving city-girl, I was completely in awe of her.

'Come up to the house tomorrow, about ten o'clock,' Carly told me. 'I'll have Bay ready for you.'

My sister hardly said a word, she just stood there, eyes wide, chewing her lip. I could not believe my luck.

My parents were dubious about the idea, but with some persuasion they agreed. 'I'll come up to the house with you,' Mum said. 'Just to meet Carly and check it'll all be ok.'

'Of course *it'll all be ok*.' I assured her, trying to conceal the irritation in my voice. What could possibly go wrong? Nothing but nothing was going to stop me riding Bay around the countryside tomorrow morning.

We walked up the drive towards the house the next day. The sun was already heating up, but there was a nice morning breeze. Perfect riding conditions. Luckily, I had brought my riding gear on holiday in the hope that an amazing opportunity such as this would arise. I never, in my wildest dreams, anticipated it would be this amazing though. So I wore my jodhpurs and a brown t-shirt with the word *Bistro* and a little row of cafés embroidered on it. Mum had brushed my hair into a low ponytail to accommodate my riding hat. I felt good and I thought I looked the part. Mum had bought me the jodhpurs in a sale at *'Tack'* on the outskirts of town. I was very pleased and had worn them on several occasions already, but not for horse riding until now. Carly was adjusting Bay's saddle when we walked into the yard at the front of Newell Hall. She turned and waved to us. 'Hi, come on, jump up and I'll fix your stirrups.'

There was a set of steps next to the horse, I had not had that luxury before. I was used to heaving myself up with one foot in a stirrup and a horse that walked away in the process. This was so much easier, and once sitting on Bay's back I felt on top of the world. Carly assured my mum that I would be fine. 'Bay is a gentle lad,' she said. 'He will look after her.' And so, reassured by that, Mum turned to go back to the cottage, and as she went down the path, she turned and blew me a kiss with her ruby red lips and smiled, her ditsy pink dress and blonde curls blowing in the breeze.

Carly showed me the route I should take. She walked with me and Bay down the drive and a little way along the road to a wheatfield opposite.

'I like your jodhpurs,' she commented, and I told her we had bought them for five pounds in the sale at *Tack*. She smiled at this and said what a great bargain they were.

14

'I'll leave you here then,' she said after we had done a lap around the edge of the field. 'Will you be alright? Go around three or four times and come back up to the house then. Is that ok?'

'Yes' I said. I couldn't wait to get going, to be alone with Bay and imagine he was my own. I felt like Elizabeth Taylor in *National Velvet*. I squeezed gently with my knees and urged Bay to quicken his pace. But he was certainly not *The Pie* and his half-hearted trot soon dissipated into a slow plod. This was not quite what I had in mind. But it was fine because I was enjoying myself so much anyway. I talked and sang to the horse, and he seemed to like it, pricking his ears back and forth to hear better. The sun beat down mercilessly as we went round and round the yellow wheatfield. I began to worry that Bay might be too hot and in need of a drink. So we finished our last lap of the field and headed towards the open gate. As Bay and I stepped out onto the road a red sports car came screaming around the bend towards us. I pulled the reins hard so that Bay backed up again into the field. The car zoomed past us at a ridiculous speed, windows down, music blaring, one man driving by the look of it. He waved his arm out the window and shouted something incoherent as he sped by. 'Idiot,' I said, rolling my eyes like Dad does when he's been cut up on the motorway. I patted Bay and urged him along the road, quickly turning into the lane which led to Newell Farm.

As we entered the gates into the grounds of the hall, I was surprised to see the red car, which had just nearly mown us down, parked in front of the house. Carly was standing on the other side of it apparently talking to the driver. She looked up briefly and smiled at me, said something to the man still sitting in the car, and then walked over. 'Was he good?' she asked, rubbing Bay's nose. Her eyes were strangely red and puffy like she had an allergy or had been crying for days. She held Bay's head while I dismounted. 'He was great,' I replied, and I was about to elaborate when the red car veered past behind me and disappeared out of the gate. Carly's red eyes followed it, her attention was no longer on Bay or me, just the car with its idiotic occupant.

 'So, we went round and round the field and it was great.' I related my Elizabeth Taylor experience to my family when I returned to the cottage. 'And Carly said she liked my jodhpurs. I told her we bought them at *Tack*.'

'You didn't tell her they cost a fiver, did you?' Dad asked.

'Yes, I did. She thought they were a great bargain.'

Mum rolled her eyes and groaned, but I didn't understand why. 'Anyway,' I continued, 'Bay was lovely and we went round the wheatfield about four times.'

'It sounds *awful* boring,' my sister commented. Dad snorted with laughter and then coughed loudly, trying to cover it up.

'No it wasn't boring. Oh you wouldn't understand. You just stick with Sindy.' I stormed off to get changed.

'I think it sounds wonderful,' Mum followed me to the bedroom. 'I would have loved to do what you did today when I was your age.' She sat on the bed as I struggled to get out of

16

my jodhpurs. 'Although, I did have a riding holiday once on the South Downs, many years ago with your Aunty Jean.'

I sighed because I had heard this story a million times already. But I let her relate it again while I changed into my white *broderie anglaise* dress.

'...and Jean had organised it all herself as a surprise. Oh, it was wonderful. I'll never forget it.' Mum ended the tale, her eyes misty with reminiscence.

I finished tying up my espadrilles. 'Ok I'm ready now,' I said.

We took a drive into the Cheviot hills that afternoon with another egg and cress picnic and parked up a rough track to admire the heat-hazy view and have a little walk in the countryside. None of us wore suitable footwear, or suitable clothes for that matter. We were townies through and through. But, despite the baking sun and uneven ground, we managed a short walk along a stony path before retreating back to the Cortina to eat our picnic in the narrow shade of a hedgerow.

'Ah this is the life,' Dad said, stretching his legs out and lighting a cigarette. And we all agreed that it was the life. But inside me there was something else that said: *Make the most of this life, because it can change in an instant and you can never go back.*

17

Chapter 2

The following day, the forecast was promising beach weather again, and so Mum packed up a tuna picnic this time, for another jaunt to Seahouses. We arrived about lunchtime and decided to have a walk round the town before heading to the beach for our picnic. It was busy with holidaymakers clogging up the narrow streets with their buckets, spades and fishing nets, and we were no exception. Down by the beach, Mum and Dad sat on some rocks watching the tide rolling in and out while my sister and I fished in the rock pools.

And it was then that I noticed Carly a little way off lying on the sand. She was with someone, a man. They lay side by side on their fronts, he had one leg stretched over one of hers. Their heads were close, his, a mass of black unruly curls and her hair tied up in its usual ponytail. I couldn't be sure, but I thought he was the man who drove the red car. They were some distance away, but I could see they were talking, and occasionally she would throw her head back laughing as if he'd said something incredibly funny. And he was stroking her tanned back and tugging at her bikini strap. She strained her arm back, swatting his hand away. Seeing them there, like that, evoked some memory of a photo story I'd read in Jackie magazine once.

She looked happy, Carly, on the beach that day. But I remembered how red her eyes were when I took Bay back to the hall after our first outing. And I thought, if this was the idiotic red car man, how come he can make her cry and laugh within the space of two days? There was something about the beach, the half-dressed bodies slow-roasting in the sun, the scent of Ambre Solaire in the air and the warm breath of a breeze on my own bare legs that gave me a funny feeling which, in turn, got me thinking about Donny Osmond. It was a deliciously unfulfilled feeling, the promise of something that, as yet, I had no knowledge of. Puberty in all its glorious confusion of lust and innocence.

My sister found a little stone, blue and speckled with gold. We examined it, and thought it was perfect; smooth and oval shaped like a tiny blue duck egg or something. 'I think the specks are copper,' Dad said, 'and look, it has a tiny hole running all the way through.' And so it did, we could not work out what must have caused that.

'Perhaps the stone formed around something, and it has taken twenty million years to make this beautiful gem with a perfect little hole right through the middle,' Mum suggested.

'It formed on the seabed around one long golden strand of mermaid's hair which had fallen there when she was brushing it with her cuttlefish comb,' said Dad. My sister and I thought it was a magical idea and quite funny that Dad, of all people, should think up such a thing. Mum smiled and gazed at him like she'd just realised he could actually be both amusing and romantic at the same time. My sister bought a piece of narrow gold ribbon and threaded the stone for Mum to wear as a necklace. It looked perfect against Mum's pale smooth skin and she told my sister that she loved her new pendant and was never going to take it off.

The next few days were spent sightseeing at all the local tourist hot spots; Holy Island with its castle and ruined priory; Bamburgh, where, at last, we swam in the sea and marvelled at the mighty castle towering above us; Dunstanburgh and Craster where we soaked up the aroma of smoking fish and walked along the rugged coastline to the castle. Castles, tea-shops, sea-swimming, souvenir shops and fish suppers galore, our holiday was everything a twelve-year-old could wish for. And horse riding too, which was the icing on the cake for me.

Before we knew it, we were into the second week of our holiday. Monday started with another ride on Bay. 'I hope the weather holds for the rest of your holiday,' Carly smiled up at me as she adjusted the stirrups. The morning was bright and warm already as I urged Bay down the drive and across the road to our wheatfield. But today, for some reason I took the first turning by mistake instead of the second. Bay knew the route to the field, but he too must have been still half asleep. The path took us into the square behind the row of terraced cottages owned by the Newells. Realising my mistake, I steered Bay around the dusty, cobbled square to go back to the road.

Two children sat on the steps of one cottage eating bowls of breakfast cereal. They stared as we passed by, and I was pleased to have an audience, no matter how young, who thought that Bay was my horse. Reaching the end of the terrace I realised there was someone else sitting on the steps of the last cottage in the row. I knew by the mess of black curls that it was Carly's *red car man*. He sat there in a dark blue vest and shorts, leaning forward on his outspread tanned legs, smoking a cigarette. His eyes seemed to be fixed on me and Bay. I felt nervous, not knowing whether to pretend I hadn't seen him, which was a physical impossibility, or smile and wave, w*oohoo hello! You don't know me but I'm the girl you nearly ran down last week, how are you?* No, that was not appropriate either.

But as we drew nearer, my problem was solved when the man stubbed out his cigarette and flicked the butt into a flower bed. He seemed not to have even seen me and Bay, or if he had, then he'd not registered us. Then he stood and turned to walk back into the cottage. It was then I noticed a young woman standing just inside the doorway, slouching against the doorframe. And as the man went inside, he seemed to push past her as if she was invisible. She stumbled, swore and steadied herself against the wall. Then she grabbed the door to slam it shut, but just as she did so, she looked out and caught my eye for a second. Only a second, but in that moment, I saw both sadness and anger in her eyes, and something else that I just couldn't quite put my finger on.

I squeezed Bay's sides with my knees to quicken his pace. I felt disconcerted at seeing that man, something about him made me feel uneasy. Turning at the end of the terrace, we passed the red car which was parked up at the side of the last cottage. I glanced inside as we went by. The upholstery was shiny black, and a blue beach towel with a picture of a yellow yacht on it was spread out across the back seat, a smiley-face air freshener hung from the rearview mirror, and I noticed a bottle of *Charlie* perfume heating up nicely on the dashboard. I was fascinated to know who the *red car man* really was. Was he on holiday or did he live in the Newell cottage? How could Carly know him so well if he was just a holidaymaker? Perhaps it was a holiday romance such as the one in my Jackie photo story. But how could they be having a holiday romance if he was married to that woman in the doorway? I was sure they *must* be married because he was wearing a vest so early in the morning. Perhaps they were all in a *love triangle*, I had read about those on Cathy and Claire's problem page.

22

I was mulling over all of this as I returned with Bay to the hall and Carly greeted me with her wide, sunny smile. 'Have you got time to pop round to the garden with me?' she asked. 'I have something for you, well for you and your family really. Come and see.' She didn't wait for an answer but led Bay around to the stable where I helped her to take off his saddle and bridle. 'I'll give him a brush later,' she said. 'Come on.' So, I followed as she walked briskly round the back of the house. The gardens swept downhill to a little stream and a beautiful view of the countryside beyond. We crossed the lawn to the far side of the house where Carly took me through a little gate and into a walled vegetable garden.

'I've been cultivating this garden for the past year,' she told me. 'It had gone to rack and ruin since Mummy died three years ago. It was her pride and joy, but I'm ashamed to say we didn't look after it very well till now. I was away a lot overseas and poor Daddy didn't have the stomach for it.' She took me for a walk along the pathways which wove around the neat vegetable beds. There, I admired the tall and leafy runner bean plants, sweet peas, strawberries, lettuce, cabbages, peppers and a little row of apple trees. And in the centre was a large deep hole, half dug. 'What's that going to be?' I asked.

'Oh it's going to be a pond, eventually,' Carly smiled, '-if Max ever finishes it that is. He's my- a friend, well, a farmworker really, but he's helped us a lot with this garden. The pond, hmm- it's taking a while. We'll get there, yeah, I hope so anyway.' She looked thoughtful. 'Mummy never had a pond here, she would have loved one.'

'It will be amazing,' I said enthusiastically, and added: 'the whole garden is brilliant, I really like it.' I had no interest whatsoever in gardening. Dad did all the gardening at home, I enjoyed being in it, playing ball games with Joni and sunbathing, but I didn't do anything to help keep it nice. Here in Carly's walled garden though, I could see that it all looked very pretty, everything growing nicely and that was the main thing. But I was more interested in who Max was. He *must* be *red car man* I decided. 'Does Max stay in one of the cottages across the road?' I surprised myself, but I had to know. Carly looked taken aback, she faltered. 'Well, er- yes, he lives there,' she said. 'Do you know him?'

'Only because he nearly ran me over one day in his red sports car.'

Carly seemed shocked at first but then relaxed a little, 'oh gosh that's awful, but it sounds like Max. He's a bit of an idiot in that car.'

I chewed my lip and nodded, thinking *great minds think alike.* Carly smiled, 'c'mon,' she said, and continued along the narrow paths between the beds with me following in her *Charlie*-scented wake. She stopped near the sweet peas. 'I've bagged up some veg for you. Give it to your mum,' she picked up a large brown paper bag and handed it to me. It was full of green beans (my least favourite), carrots, strawberries, courgettes, onions and tomatoes. I thanked her very much as it

24

was very kind of her to think of us. Mum said the same later when I handed her the bag. 'I'll make us a lovely vegetable stew for dinner,' she said, laying out the produce on the table to inspect.

'Oooh wonderful, we can't wait can we girls?' Dad rolled his eyes grinning at us kids. We both smirked and my sister faked vomiting. We all knew that when Mum said she was making something 'lovely' for dinner, our worst food nightmare was about to come true. In the end the stew wasn't bad I had to admit. Perhaps it was the freshness of the vegetables or the fact that Carly had grown them. So we went to bed, full and sleepy, looking forward to another hot and sultry day ahead.

And on cue, the day dawned bright and warm, and the next, and the next. The summer went down in meteorological and cultural history as one of the hottest summers ever. I was glad I had talked Mum into buying me a wardrobe of bright T-shirts and shorts and running up a few dresses for the holiday, all similar to clothes I had seen on Jackie's fashion pages. I remember them to this day, the leg o' mutton sleeves, the groovy collars, the hotpants, I felt like the bees knees. None of it suitable for walking in the countryside, but ok for mooching around Seahouses and hanging out on the beach.

And then, suddenly, it seemed our holiday was drawing to a close. There were only three days left and I was beginning to feel the sense of dread that comes with the threat of school looming. I tried to put it out of my mind and enjoy the time I had left, and I knew then, how Ann Boleyn must have felt, trying to enjoy her last days before the execution.

'God you're so dramatic,' said my sister when I told her my thoughts. 'Going to school is nothing like getting your head chopped off.'

'I know that, but the feeling of dread is similar. Trying to make the most of your last days with an awful feeling of doom hanging over you. That's what I meant.'

'Oh, I see,' she said and continued drawing biro eyeliner on Sindy.

'You'll never get that off,' I warned her.

'I won't want to; she's going to look brilliant.'

Chapter 3

On the second to last day of our holiday I woke to the *craw craw* of rooks circling the trees at the top of the horse's field, and sunlight filtering through the chintz curtains. I had no idea what the day would bring. If I had, I would have packed all our things single-handedly and insisted on going home right there and then. Over the intervening years I have gone through every detail of that day, the second to last day of our holiday, a million times. The rooks, the light, my parents raised voices in

26

the kitchen, the gentle breathing of my sleeping sister. If only time had stopped still. If only they hadn't argued. If only, if only, if only.

My sister and I were ready to go. I had woken her up and we'd both dressed quickly, eaten breakfast and gathered our costumes, goggles and fishing nets, eager to go to the beach. Now we sat on the wall outside the cottage, smoking sweet cigarettes and waiting. I took a long suck on mine and chewed a little off the end. 'Oh Lord, Lizzie, what on earth's taking them so bloody long?' said my Princess Margaret to the Queen.

'Gawd knows. Having a bloody awful tiff I suppose,' the Queen replied, dragging on her fake ciggie. And we both burst into fits of laughter. The front door slammed, and we jumped down off the wall, swallowing our sweet ciggie butts and picking up our swimming things.

'Mum's not coming,' Dad said curtly, unlocking the car. 'She's got a headache, she's staying here. I'll take you to the beach. Come on.'

I was not really bothered that Mum wasn't coming, as long as we got to go swimming although I was a bit worried that we didn't have a picnic. 'Shall we say goodbye?' I asked.

'No, get in the car,' he insisted. 'You'll see her later.'

This was unusual. Mum was the leader in our family, she was the organiser. Even if she had a headache would take an aspirin, paint her lips red and carry on. That was her way. I had an urge to go back into the cottage and see her, say goodbye, tell her I'd see her later. But dad wasn't in the mood for delays, he was in the mood where he must not be argued with. So I didn't go back. I wish I had. How I wish I had.

Dad took us to the beach at Bamburgh where my sister and I spent the day swimming and running in and out of the waves. The air was oppressive and the sky thick with cloud. Dad sat on the sand chain-smoking and staring out to sea. He didn't say much all day and we were having too much fun in the water to ask if anything was wrong. Later, we bought fish and chips in the village and ate them in the car park by the castle. It was about six o'clock when we headed back to Newell Farm.

When we went into the cottage all was quiet. Dad threw his car keys on the kitchen table and went into the lounge. I followed him, my sister behind me. There was a piece of paper on the coffee table, a handwritten note.

'She's gone to Seahouses,' he said.

'Why?' I asked.

'Oh I don't know,' Dad sat on the small, green sofa and leaned forward, his head in his hands.

'Perhaps she's gone to get some tea for herself,' my sister suggested.

'Yes love, perhaps,' he held out a hand to her and she went to sit on his lap.

I didn't know what to make of it. Seahouses was not far in the car, but it would be a long way to walk.

'Maybe we should go in the car and get her,' I said.

'We could do, I suppose,' Dad agreed. So we drove to Seahouses, all around the town two or three times and back along the road to Newell Farm. But there was no sign of Mum anywhere.

I looked out the car window on the way back as the fields sped by and a hundred swallows dipped and dived in the evening sun. The wheatfield where I had ridden Bay so many times glowed golden, but everything seemed to have lost its magical holiday vibe. Suddenly everything felt shadowed and tainted with worry. *Where is she?* I wondered, scanning the countryside.

'She might be back now, in the cottage,' my sister said, as though she'd read my thoughts.

'Maybe,' I replied hoping she was right.

But to our dismay, she was wrong. Mum wasn't back and she didn't come back all night. Or the next morning. And then, things started to seem a lot more serious. Dad went up to Newell Hall. 'You stay here girls, I won't be long,' he said, pulling on his jacket. 'I need to use the telephone.' He patted me on the shoulder, 'look after your sister, don't go out, just wait here for me.'

'Ok Dad,' I said, feeling responsible. 'We'll be alright.'

He was back within half an hour and Carly was with him. She was wearing a yellow t-shirt with *Chelsea Girl* written on it, white shorts and green-flash tennis shoes. I was impressed, but not as much as usual because Mum was taking up most of my thoughts.

29

'Hi girls,' she said in a sympathetic tone. 'How are you doing? Would you like to come up to the house with me? We can feed Bay, he's in his stable.'

I looked at my sister and then at Dad. 'Yes,' he said, 'you go along with Carly. Some people are coming I need to talk to. People who are going to help us find Mum.'

'Police people?' I asked.

'Yes,' dad said quietly.

Why didn't he just say *police?* I wondered as we left the cottage with Carly. Trying to soften the blow by saying *'some people'* I supposed, but it hadn't helped. The blow was still hard. Now this was a *police matter* as they'd say in Z Cars. My mother was a police matter. I could hardly believe it.

My sister and I held hands as we walked up to Newell Hall. We very rarely held hands, only if we absolutely had to, like when crossing a very busy road or doing the hokey-cokey at a party. But it seemed more appropriate than ever right now.

'Where do you think Mum has gone?' She whispered to me, her big brown eyes pleading for an answer.

'I don't know,' I said and squeezed her hand. 'But don't worry. She'll turn up.'

She'll turn up like a lost cat who got trapped in someone's shed, or a lost glove that someone picks up and leaves on a gatepost. She's a grown woman, she can't be lost, grown people don't get lost, they find their way somehow, with a map or by asking a stranger. She's just lost to us because we don't know where she is. But she might not think she's lost.

She might be sitting in a café in Seahouses having a cup of coffee, not even realising that she's causing such a fuss.

So we waited with Carly and fed Bay a bucket of oats and gave him a brush. And Carly took us into the huge kitchen at Newell Hall and made us some pancakes. Any other time I would have been in seventh heaven but now- now my heart wasn't in it. It was heavy with fear and trepidation. We waited up at the hall for what seemed like hours. Then, I heard men's voices in the hall. Mr. Newell's booming one said: 'The cottage is booked up from Saturday, but if you need to stay longer, you can stay here at the house. That won't be a problem. Free of charge of course. I'm so sorry my good man, about this whole rotten thing. Bloody awful business.'

And my dad's quiet one saying: 'That's very good of you Mr. Newell, thank you. We might need a couple more days. Police said it's a missing person case. They're not suspicious yet. I don't know why not. She wouldn't leave her kids; I know she wouldn't.'

'Of course, of course. Well come along inside and let's get you a whisky. I should think you need it.' They came into the room where my sister and I were doing a jigsaw with Carly. Dad sat next to me. He put an arm around me and reached the other one out to hold my sister's hand. 'Good girls,' he said, and his voice was thick and choked like he had a bad cold, but when I looked up, he was crying. I'd never seen him cry before and I couldn't really understand why he was crying now.

Mum had gone to Seahouses, it wasn't the end of the world. Yes, she was taking longer than you'd expect but- *but what?* That was the question, a big almighty *but* that no one could answer. *But-* it was nice in Seahouses, and she'd decided to stay overnight in a guest house, get a bit of peace and quiet. *But-* she'd had a row with Dad, and it was a good opportunity to teach him a lesson. *But-* she'd spent the past twelve years of her life looking after us and now she wanted to escape, disappear into the sunset on a fishing boat to the Farne islands with some weather-beaten fisherman. Clearly, Dad hadn't thought of these scenarios. He was crying because he couldn't bear to be apart from her even just for one night. But I knew it would all be alright in the end. Mum would return and tell us all exactly what happened and give us an answer to the big almighty *but.*

That night we stayed at Groom's cottage because we had one day left of our holiday. I expected Mum to turn up at any moment. She would breeze through the door with a bright smile on her red lips and her blonde curls bouncing on her shoulders. She would throw her little yellow handbag down and gather us up in her arms and say how sorry she was for all the worry she'd caused us. 'I just had to get away for a while,' she would say. 'You will forgive me, won't you? I was a fool to stay away so long.' And we will hug her and say, *'of course* we forgive you!' And then I realised my pillow was wet and I was actually crying because I was so desperate for that scenario to become reality. It was like when I longed for

32

Donny Osmond to be my boyfriend. No amount of imagining could bring that to reality either.

All day we hung around waiting. Just waiting. My sister and I spent a while in the field stroking the horses that morning. Dad sat at the kitchen table with his head in his hands mostly. Then he walked up to Newell Hall to make a few phone calls. 'I need to tell Aunty Jean' he said, 'can't put it off any longer.' While he was gone, my sister and I sat on the front wall. We'd been told by Dad not to leave the cottage, so technically we were within our rights as the wall belonged to the cottage. As we sat there, the red car turned into the drive. But instead of speeding like he usually did, the idiot drove slowly along, past our wall. His window was open, and he was staring at us. So, for the first time, I got quite a good look at him. He was dirty looking with a stubbly chin, dark curly hair which was held back by the sunglasses perched on his head. He had a blue, open necked shirt on and a cigarette hanging out of his mouth. He was actually quite handsome, but he needed a good wash and brush up. Our eyes met, his were pale blue, made more noticeable because his skin was so tanned. I didn't know how to look away without appearing rude or weak or something, I had been brought up with manners which I was compelled to act upon even in the most unusual of circumstances. But I wished I could have avoided the strange smirk on his face. I didn't know why he would smirk at me, but he did, I'm sure of it. It made me feel small and uncomfortable, as if he knew something I didn't. Then he revved his engine and sped off up the drive to the hall.

'Creep' said my sister, and it was exactly the right word.

Dad returned from the hall looking drained. 'Aunty Jean was upset on the phone,' he told us. 'We're going up to Newell Hall tomorrow, we'll stay there a couple of days till we get some news off the- the police.'

Poor Aunty Jean was Mum's older sister. She was less glamorous, less vivacious than Mum. Down to earth and practical, *frumpy* some might say, but she was good to us. She never married or had children of her own. Mum told us she had a lovely soldier boyfriend during the war, but he was killed on D-Day. So I always felt very sorry for her and mentally forgave her if she told me off about anything because I think she deserved a bit of leeway.

That evening we packed our bags while Dad made rock hard fish fingers, mash and beans for tea. He was not a great cook, but it was edible- just.

'Do you think mother will come back, Maggie?' asked the Queen.

'Gawd knows Lizzie. Try and get some sleep.'

'But she'd have a terrible time if she doesn't come back soon. She'll have to get the bloody train home with all the riff raff.'

I lay on my back examining the pink nylon tasseled lampshade above me.

'She's not going to miss coming home with us Lizzie.' I picked up a pencil from my bedside table to use as a ciggie and pretended to inhale deeply from it. 'Anyway, if she does have to get the train, we'll just wait for her back at the palace. We'll get the bloody G&Ts ready.' I blew out the fake smoke so hard it rocked the lampshade.

My sister smiled and turned on her side to face me. Then a cloud came down and her eyes closed. 'What if she never comes back?'

'Don't,' I said, 'she will come back. She wouldn't leave us.'

I couldn't get excited about staying at Newell Hall. We were only going there because Mum was missing and that fact over-rode any chance of excitement. It wasn't something you could forget about, even for a minute. Dad packed Mum's things in the suitcase they shared, her dresses, her perfume, her shoes, everything. I didn't see him do it, I couldn't bear to look at her clothes and I was glad that I didn't have to. It seemed strange packing the car up with all our stuff just to drive two minutes up to the hall and unload it all again.

Carly was there to greet us. 'Hello there,' she walked towards the car with her head tilted and a subdued smile. She managed to sound welcoming, sympathetic and pleased to see us all in one. She had a knack, Carly, of hitting just the right note for the given situation including this, the most unlikely one of all. She took us through the hallway and up the wide curving staircase to show us our rooms. My sister and I were sharing a room and Dad would be in the one next door. He patted Carly's arm as she opened his door for him. 'I can't thank you enough,' he said in a wavering voice. She placed her hand on

35

his, 'no no, not at all,' she said. 'I just wish you were staying under happier circumstances.'

I couldn't help thinking that we wouldn't be staying at all if we were under happier circumstances. We would be going home today instead with Mum. And I wished that was the case despite this golden opportunity to stay for free at Newell Hall with Carly.

That afternoon the police came to see Dad. He told us to wait in our bedroom. I wanted to hear what the police had to say but Dad wouldn't let me. 'It'll just be an update. I'll tell you what they say, love,' he said. I wasn't satisfied with that but there was nothing I could do save for eavesdropping at the door. So I watched from the banisters as Dad and the policemen disappeared into a downstairs room, and I sneaked down to eavesdrop at the door. It was hard to hear because the door was made of thick oakwood, so I pressed my ear to the keyhole. I could hear the voices of the police asking a succession of questions. *Can you remember what she was wearing that morning? Do you know what she took with her? Did you know she was having an affair Mr. Fisher?* But before I could hear Dad's responses, I felt a touch on my shoulder. It was Carly. 'Come on Billie,' she said, 'let's go and get something to eat.'

Mum had called me Billie after Billie Holiday. When I was about ten years old, I hated my name because no other girl was called Billie. Then, about two years later I loved my name, because no other girl was called Billie. She sang the blues, in the kitchen, my mum, when she was cooking, or sipping her Martini and soda, or just looking out the window at the alleyway and the back to backs. And Billie's quivering, heartbroken voice would accompany her. Then she would turn to me, her eyes shining and that red-lipstick smile spreading across her face. And she'd grab my hands and we would sway around the kitchen to *That Ole Devil Called Love*.

Mum and Dad were sociable people. They loved throwing a dinner party or a full-on roll-back-the-carpet party for a birthday or Halloween or Christmas, or for no reason at all, other than they just felt like it. We loved the anticipation, the preparation and the excitement. On one occasion, when I was about eleven, Dad had some colleagues from work round for dinner. Three men and two women. They were a raucous bunch, eating, smoking, drinking and getting louder and louder as the night went on. One of them, a man probably in his fifties with a tweed jacket and handlebar moustache, was snorting something from a small metal box. I had no idea what that was all about, but everyone seemed to find it hilarious. 'Oh, good Lord, Frank, I thought that went out with the ark,' exclaimed one of the women. He offered the box for others to try. My sister and I were chased off to bed at this stage before things got any worse. It was later when I got up to use the loo that I heard a funny noise coming from the spare room. I pushed the door open and saw that man Frank with my mother. She was standing by the wall, and he was pushing up against her and kissing her. She had one leg bent up, her flowery dress falling back to reveal her stocking top and his fat red hand on her thigh. She turned her head as I let the light into the room and saw me. She moved very fast then and pushed Frank sharply away from her. He stumbled and fiddled with his trousers. I backed out of the room quickly and locked myself in the bathroom.

I wasn't sure what I'd seen but I knew I didn't like it. I could hear urgent whispers on the landing and footsteps going down the stairs. When I went back to my room Mum was sitting on my bed. 'Oh Billie love,' she said, 'please forget you saw Frank and me like that. We were very silly. Sometimes grown-ups do silly things, especially when they've been drinking alcohol.' She stroked my hair back off my face. I looked at her with her red lipstick smeared around her mouth and black smudges under her eyes. And I thought *adults like that word 'silly'. They use it to try and make serious things seem trivial.* 'Okay,' I said. 'I won't tell Dad.' Mum looked relieved and sad and ashamed. Or maybe I just imagined the whole thing, I hoped so.

Now, in Carly's kitchen, eating a ham sandwich, I wondered again about Frank and Mum, and the incident which I had cast into the uncharted recesses of my twelve-year-old brain. *Did you know she was having an affair, Mr. Forest?* I knew, but I never spoke about it. I badly wanted to be wrong, but it turned out I was right. When the police left, Dad came to talk to my sister and me. 'They haven't found her I'm afraid. But they'll keep looking for her. They've asked people at home if anyone's seen her, her friends, you know. And Aunty Jean.'

'But no-one's seen her?' my sister asked, her voice subdued.

'No darling, no-one at home has. So she's probably still nearby.'

The thought lifted my spirits. *She's still nearby*. Perhaps she can even see us from where she is. Maybe she's camping out in the copse of trees at the top of the hill. And then I realised what a ridiculous idea that was, Mum was terrified of insects. She would never camp, not in a million years.

That evening Carly made us dinner using fresh vegetables from the walled garden and fish in a lovely creamy sauce. It was the best meal we'd had for days. We all sat together with Mr. Newell in the dining room. Conversation was a bit uneasy. Dad was lost in his own thoughts and my sister looked like she might fall asleep into her dinner. No one else seemed to know what to say, after all we were thrown together by the strangest of circumstances. We really didn't know each other at all.

'This fish is really nice,' I piped up eventually.

'Oh,' Carly turned to me smiling, 'I'm glad you like it.'

'What do you think we'll do tomorrow Dad?' I asked.

He finished his mouthful of food and said 'I don't know love. Not a lot, I have to be available in case the police need to speak to me.'

'That is absolutely fine,' Mr. Newell interrupted. 'You can stay here, use the house and garden as you like. We have a small library if you like to read. Do you like to read?' he turned to me.

'Oh yes,' I answered 'do you have any Enid Blyton?'

'I'm sure I have some old Enid Blyton books somewhere,' Carly offered. 'I'll have a look in the morning.'

I felt bad about all the times Dad had cursed Mr. Newell for waking us so early, directing the farmworkers outside Groom's cottage. Now he was being so kind and understanding. I liked him, I thought he was actually a very nice man. And that was how the evening went. We ate and talked about nothing much and there were long gaps in the conversation, but it was alright. That was enough for us.

The next morning, I slept till ten o'clock and woke to find a small pile of Enid Blyton books outside my door. My sister was not in her bed, and I assumed she must be downstairs with Dad or Carly. I took the books back to bed and read for the rest of the morning. I must have fallen asleep again and when I woke, I could hear noises from outside. Looking out, I realised that my window overlooked the walled garden where Max was working. I washed and dressed quickly and went to find Dad and Joni who were playing cards downstairs. I read all day and ate Carly's blueberry pancakes, there was not much else to do. Outside it was still hot, but I didn't dare go in the garden for fear of running into that idiot Max.

There was no more contact from the police that day, or the next. Dad rang them himself on Monday. But still, they had no news about Mum. 'Police say we might as well go home; they can reach us there.' Dad looked exhausted and worried. I wished Mum were here to look after him, but then he wouldn't be like this if she was here. And hadn't had an affair. After dinner we packed our things ready for an early start the next day. I dreaded leaving without Mum. Two weeks ago, when we arrived here full of excitement, no-one dreamed our holiday would end this way. I felt like we were leaving her behind, abandoning her. I thought my heart was breaking.

Chapter 4

Home is where the heart is, they reckon. But the heart had been pulled out of ours. Mum was gone, she hadn't come back even though I had prayed harder for that than anything ever before, harder even, than I'd prayed for Donny Osmond to be my boyfriend. Now, three weeks after our return from holiday we were still motherless, wifeless- and, if we include Frank in the equation, loverless.

The papers were on it now:

Cheating Wife Disappears on Holiday
Family left Bereft by Cheating Wife
Children Abandoned by Cheating Mother

Take your pick of headlines, well- page two lines, but not bad for an otherwise ordinary family with no other claims to fame.

'Why do they say *cheating*?' asked my sister at the breakfast table.

'Good God,' Dad spluttered over his cornflakes. 'How does she know that? Billie? Where did she hear that?'

'I don't know,' I lied.

She'd seen it at the sweet shop when we went for my Jackie. We'd spent a little time perusing the papers on the bottom shelf.

'Bloody hell.' Dad murmured. 'Listen, Joni,' (after Joni Mitchell) 'forget about what the papers say. They talk rubbish. You just need to listen to me, that's all. We love your mum. We still love her, and we'll be here when she decides to come back.'

'We still love her even though she was cheating?' Joni continued.

'Yes. No. *Yes*, of course we love her. Just- just forget about the cheating. Oh God.' He got up, kissed us each on the cheek and went into the hall where he put on his jacket and his helmet for the long drive to work.

'I'll see you later,' he called on his way out the front door. 'Aunty Jean will be here soon.'

Joni picked the straw out of her milk cup and held it in her mouth like a cigarette, then blew out, long and hard. 'What did Mother cheat at Maggie? For *Christ's* sake darling, do tell one.'

'She cheated at love, Lizzie. I think that's what it means. It's bloody complicated. I don't *raarhly* understand it myself to be quite honest.' I tried to be light-hearted, but I just wasn't feeling it. I shovelled a spoonful of cornflakes into my mouth.

Joni said, 'but we still love her, and we'll be here when she decides to come back. That's what Dad said.' She swished the straw around in her milk.

'Yep. That's what Dad said,' I agreed.

But it was about then, I think, that I knew Mum couldn't come back. There was no *deciding* about it. This knowledge seemed to have grown slowly within me, like a little shoot of ivy climbing its way inexorably up and around and in and out, strangling the life out of any hope I had left.

Dear Cathy and Claire

I hope you can print this letter and help me with my unusual problem. You see, my mum had an affair even though she was still

43

married to my dad. I thought they were happy together. I hoped it wasn't true about the affair, but it was. Then she disappeared when we were on holiday. We haven't seen her for four weeks now. The other man, Frank (who she had the affair with) is still here, at Dad's work. So we know she didn't run away with him. Have you any ideas about what might have happened to her? I would be very grateful for your advice.

Thank you.

Billie Fisher

Dad was sent home from work that day after punching Frank in the face.

'Not very clever,' commented Aunty Jean with characteristic understatement.

'It wasn't meant to be clever.'

'Oh well. That's alright then I suppose, teaching your girls to sort out a problem with their fists.'

Dad ignored that, he sighed loudly and opened a beer from the fridge.

'I wouldn't punch anyone, Aunty Jean,' said Joni.

'I'm glad to hear it love.'

'I would if I had to,' I said.

Aunty Jean raised an eyebrow. 'Well let's hope you never have to.'

'It was worth it to see the look on his smug, fat face.' Dad sat at the kitchen table and took a swig of his beer. I grinned; I was quite proud of him.

'Right, that's enough talk of punching and fat faces,' Aunty Jean said, pulling on her coat. 'Since you're back now Ronnie, I'll be off. Are you going to work tomorrow for another bout? Do you need me here?'

'I'm off till Monday now, I've been told. So we're ok till then. Thanks Jean. Sorry, you know- about- all that.' Dad looked suitably sheepish. Aunty Jean relented and ran her hand over his shoulder, brushing off some invisible dandruff and patting him gently. She bent and kissed his cheek. Then she kissed Joni and me and left.

Because of our situation and all the hoo-ha with the newspapers, school let Dad decide when it was the right time for Joni and me to go back. It was coming to the end of September when he felt the time was right. I didn't agree but he was adamant.

'We can't expect Aunty Jean to keep coming to look after you indefinitely while I go to work,' he said. 'And you're missing your lessons, you'll end up working in Leo's if you're not careful.'

'I can think of worse things,' I told him, and got a telling off for being flippant.

So, we returned to school. The Sunday before, I had that feeling of dread all day. I got my uniform ready and my bag, even just doing that plunged me into despair. Joni felt the same, but at least she was still in primary school. She could walk there and have a nice cosy day, painting and being read to on the carpet. I had to get two buses with the yobs from St. Margaret's and be yelled at by nuns all day. I missed Mum helping me get my stuff ready and making my packed lunch. I missed her saying goodbye at the front door in her quilted dressing gown, her red lips mouthing *see you later*. My friend Cheryl from the next street called for me and I had a tear in my eye. She put her arm around me for a bit and I appreciated it, but we couldn't walk far like that. In the end, it wasn't so bad going back, it took my mind off things, seeing friends again. Even the nuns seemed to be on their best behaviour.

I dreamed Mum was swimming in a circular shaped pool, it was bright and sunny and there were colourful flowers and fruits hanging down from trellises into the water. She was wearing a red swimming hat with big orange rubber flowers all over it. And she waved and smiled, beckoning me to come into the pool too. This was unusual because Mum couldn't swim, she was scared of the water. In my dream the light started fading and heavy grey clouds formed overhead. Mum looked up, her red lips stopped smiling and changed to purple. And then everything turned to black and white like an old movie. Mum looked down with an expression of horror on her face as the inky black water began to swirl fiercely around her in a terrifying whirlpool pulling her round and round, then sucking her down until her hand, reaching upwards, was the last part of her to disappear.

46

I woke up fighting for my breath as if I too were drowning. This was a recurring dream. Sometimes the details changed, she might call my name or there might be music playing in the background. But the effect was always the same. Horror, fear, tears, sleeplessness. I was exhausted with my nightly trauma and became afraid to go to sleep at all. Instead, I read. Anything I could get my hands on, Jackie of course, and Enid Blyton, and even some other authors that I hadn't tried before. I raided the library on a weekly basis, and I read and read every night until I fell into a deep sleep. But still the nightmare came. Still my mother called out night after night for me to save her. But I could not.

'So your mum is a ghost now,' our cousin Rodney said.

'Shut up you stupid idiot,' I slapped his face as hard as I could. Joni ran into the kitchen crying.

'Why did you say that?' I asked him as he clutched his reddening cheek.

'Well, you don't think she's still alive, do you? Oh, unless she's run off with *another* man,' he smirked. I raised my hand to deliver a follow-up slap, but someone caught hold of it mid-air.

'Enough of that, Billie,' I heard my dad's voice say. 'Jean was right. Hitting people isn't the way to settle your disputes.'

Dad's brother, Uncle Des, followed him into the room. 'Rodney, you little bugger, stop upsetting the girls.'

Fortunately, Uncle Des, Aunty Dawn and Rodney were very infrequent visitors. In pre-Mum's-disappearance days, we

47

rarely saw them. This recent visit was out of the blue. They said they wanted to offer support, but I couldn't see how they could support us. I thought they just wanted a mention in the papers.

Much as I had been angry over Rodney's crass comment it did get me thinking about ghosts, and Mum's ghost in particular. Was she a ghost? That would mean she had died of course. My feelings were very confused. On one hand I felt scared that she might haunt me. On the other, she was my mother, why would she want to frighten me? Then there was the desperate sadness at the thought she might be dead. But it was the ghost thing that preoccupied me. I went to bed that night and stared into the darkness, hoping to see her, but at the same time terrified that she might appear like a wailing, flailing banshee. I buried my head under the blankets and tried to think about the Famous Five. I must have fallen asleep for a while; I don't know how long. Then my eyes opened into the blackness.

It'll be alright Billie, she said.

Two months went by before the police came to see Dad again. They were in the front room for about an hour while Joni and I played in the garden wrapped up in our winter woollies. Aunty Jean was knitting in the lounge with our neighbour Mrs. Thomas. We could see them through the window, gossiping ten to the dozen.

'Bloody hell, Mrs. Thomas's jaw'll seize up if she doesn't give it a rest soon,' Joni said. We could see Aunty Joan laugh at something that Mrs. Thomas had said, then her head turned to the door as Dad came into the room. He was talking for a few minutes. We watched; Joni was bouncing a ball on her tennis racket. Then Aunty Jean put her face in her hands. Mrs. Thomas reached across her shoulder patting her back and Dad put his hand on her other shoulder.

'She's crying,' I said, and fear bloomed throughout my whole body like an icy frost across a window. Joni let the ball and racket fall to the floor and she raced back into the house.

Dear Cathy and Claire

I know you must be very busy with a lot of post and problems to reply to, so I don't mind that you didn't print my last letter. But I just wanted to update you in case you do get a chance to reply. My mother still hasn't been found. The police can't find any trace of her, and now they've closed the case. It's very hard not knowing what happened to her. I'd be very grateful for any hints or advice you can give, that might make me feel better about it.

Thank you

Billie Fisher

Chapter 5

Mum had always loved Christmas. She went to town on fairy lights and weird little ornaments, plastic rabbit heads with holly round their necks and chubby angels on sparkly half-moons. This year we didn't have the heart for Christmas. Dad dragged the box down from the loft and we opened it up one Saturday afternoon in December.

'We'll feel better when they're up,' Dad said pulling out a long piece of red tinsel. I wasn't convinced, but Joni looked hopeful.

'Let's ring Aunty Jean to come and help,' I suggested. For some reason, I just wanted her there. A motherly figure, I suppose, and someone else who knew and loved Mum to come and share our grief at putting the Christmas decorations up.

So, Aunty Jean came round, and brought with her a big fruit loaf, some hot chocolate and a bottle of sherry. In the end, it was a nice afternoon. We all ate the fruit loaf; Joni and I drank the hot chocolate and Dad and Aunty Jean got tipsy on the sherry. We put Christmas music on the record player and once the fairy lights were strung across the room, I started to feel more Christmassy and like there was a point to all this after all.

I set up the nativity set, placing the animals carefully in the stable and baby Jesus in his crib. And I said a little prayer in my head asking Him to rescue Mum or bring her back to life, whichever was needed to get her home to us. Then I shook my head because it was a stupid prayer and obviously Jesus didn't give two hoots about her, or us, or he wouldn't have let her disappear in the first place. But still, I liked the nativity set, it was peaceful and smelt comfortingly musty, and it reminded me of when I was very small, and everything seemed perfect.

Aunty Jean made us tea before she called a cab to take her home. She'd had a little too much sherry and her cooking wasn't up to her usual standard. But we weren't very hungry after all the fruit loaf, so burnt bacon on toast was enough. Dad was lounging on the sofa watching *The Golden Shot* when Joni went to bed. I decided I'd stay up a while longer and sat down with a cup of milk. Dad didn't turn around, but he said 'I'm proud of you Billie you know. You're a good girl.' I knew at this stage that all the sherry had gone to his head. But it was a nice thing to say anyway.

'Thanks Dad.'

His head lolled on the arm of the sofa. 'Yes, you're a good girl. So is Joni. I'm a lucky man, having two daughters like you. I'm sorry about all this. I really am. Your mum going off like that. It's my fault, I should have been a better husband.'

I wasn't sure I wanted to hear any more, but I couldn't think what to say. He went on. 'Your mum was too good for me.'

51

'No, Dad, don't say that. You were both good. Good for each other.'

'The police say she didn't go to Seahouses. No one saw her there. They say she never got that far.' He started crying and wiped his face with his jumper sleeve. I stayed silent, trying to make sense of what he'd said.

'She never got that far,' he repeated, and pulled a handkerchief out of his pocket. He blew his nose loudly and wiped his eyes.

'Where do they think she went then?'

'She must have met someone. Someone she knew- or, more likely, didn't know. She must have been picked up. Or she called a taxi to take her somewhere. She took her bag, but she only had a bit of cash in her purse, she never carried much money. I had our cheque book, so where would she have gone?' Dad pulled himself up and shifted around to see me better. 'Oh love, I'm sorry. I don't know why I'm telling you all this. I've had too much to drink. If Aunty Jean was still here, she'd tell me to shut up. You don't need to worry about all these details. They don't matter. She's gone. That's all there is to it.'

'Someone took her, she wouldn't have left us.' I said.

The music began. Billie Holiday singing *Blue Moon*. And then the marvellous moonlit scene came into view. Like one of those old technicolour movies, beautiful women in 1950s costumes swam in formation through huge pools filled with yellow water lilies. Ruby red lips all smiling, all having a wonderful time. The choreography was incredible, I'll never

52

know how my sleeping adolescent mind came up with all that. And then, taking centre stage of course, was Mum in her floral costume and a swimming cap covered in fruit and flowers. Slowly she descended on a bower of white lilies which was lowered gently to the water. She stepped off into the sparkling, blue pool and was surrounded by the other swimmers and water lilies and... 'Wake up Billie. You're going to be late for school,' Joni was shaking my arm. I groaned. But I was glad she'd woken me before it got to the part in the movie where the water turns into a seething whirlpool, and everyone is dragged under to their deaths.

Dear Cathy and Claire
I wrote to you a little while ago, I don't know if you remember. My mum went missing on holiday last summer. Well, she hasn't come back yet. She left a note to say she was going to the town nearby but now the police don't think she even got there at all. Do you think she will come back? In your experience do missing people usually turn up in the end? If you can advise me about this, I would be very grateful.
Thank you
Billie Fisher

Every morning before school I did Joni's long hair for her. Mum always said Joni was like Dad and I was like her. Dad only had to be out in the sun for five minutes and his skin would go brown as a nut. His hair was brown too, like Joni's, but his had gone grey at the sides and his face had developed lines in the five years since Mum went. I grew more like her every day, doing the things she used to do around the house, helping Dad, helping Joni. I was always a helpful person, Mum said. I was thinking about all this on a rainy Monday morning while I was doing Joni's hair as usual.

'Ouch, you're pulling, Joni scolded me. 'You're too rough.'

'Oh, shush and hold still,' I said, brushing the top section tightly back into a high ponytail. Carly wore a ponytail, but hers was never as neat as this. There were always stray blonde wisps escaping. I smiled remembering her that summer, in the field with Bay, before well- you know. We hadn't seen Carly since the day we left Newell Hall. That dark, dark day when we left Mum behind. Carly rang us a few times in the first year after the holiday. But, because so much time went by with nothing new to talk about, we had lost touch with the Newells.

Then Mum came back, suddenly, out of the blue. It was on my seventeenth birthday. The day started with me feeling terrible. Every birthday without Mum was a trial, but, for some reason, this one seemed the worst of all. It felt almost unbearable. I lay on my bed staring at Donny with his shining brown eyes and his gleaming smile and asked him, for the millionth time, what on earth had happened to Mum. He had no answers of course because he is not God. And even God did not seem to have any answers, or if he did, he was keeping them to himself.

I had felt her around before sometimes, quietly whispering a little word in my ear, sending me a reassuring message now and then. But, on that morning of my birthday, just as I was giving up on Donny, God and Cathy and Claire, I heard her clearly. *Happy birthday my love*, she said. That's all. Just-happy birthday my love. She had remembered, after all these years. So, I knew that she was always with me, and I felt very happy that day because of this amazing turn of events. Dad and Joni and Aunty Jean seemed surprised that I was so upbeat. Usually on my birthday there was at least one or two moments when I had been upset about Mum's absence, opening presents, or blowing out birthday candles. And there would be a little pep talk from Dad, raising my spirits in the face of adversity, and a teary moment with Aunty Jean over the washing up, that sort of thing. But this year, I felt just fine. Mum was here with me, what was there to be sad about?

I didn't tell the others, mainly because I realised that Mum was not speaking to them too. There must be a reason for that I thought. Perhaps she didn't trust them to keep it secret that she had come back. Perhaps she was scared of something. The reason for her disappearance. Maybe someone was coming after her. So, I kept quiet about it. I had to protect her.

Donny had had his day; he just wasn't cutting the mustard anymore. The poster came down. Those gleaming teeth and shining eyes were crumpled into a ball and thrown in one fabulous shot into the wastepaper bin. 'I don't need you now Donny, you're a good-looking guy but you're bloody useless.

You never showed up when I needed you. So, its c'est la vie.' Or, *what's the phrase?* I couldn't remember. '*So long sucker-* yes, that's it.' I was seventeen now, I had no need of pop idols or God or Cathy and Claire.

Oh, that waste of space, Cathy and Claire. They never answered a single letter from a desperate child. I poured my broken heart out in those letters, and they never once bothered their arses to answer any of them. Not one single word of sympathy or advice did they offer. Bitches. And then I had a thought. I bet they knew something all along, but they were keeping it to themselves. Perhaps they even knew where Mum was and what had happened to her. I bet the police and the newspapers told them not to answer my letters. It's obvious, the police and the newspapers would look pretty ridiculous if Cathy and Claire knew the truth all the time, when they hadn't been able to solve the crime. And there had been a crime, I was sure of that.

'Hey Maggie, are you in there, can one come in?' the Queen was knocking on the bathroom door.

'Yes darling, I am. Of course, come in if one wants.'

Joni came into the bathroom. I was soaking in a Radox bath. She picked up her toothbrush, took a long drag and sat on the toilet lid blowing out imaginary smoke. 'Bloody hell, its steamy in here Maggie.'

'I'm getting myself ready, Lizzie.'

'Ready for what?'

'My trip up west.'

'Your what?'

'Don't say *what* Lizzie, it's not bloody polite.'

'Oh, gosh, sorry Mags. But where are you going?'

'I'm going up west, uptown, you know. Tomorrow, I'm taking the train to the big city, London. I might pop in and say *Hi* to Charlie.'

'I see,' said Joni, but she didn't see. I could tell.

'You can come if you want,' I said.

'I don't think so, I'm going to Tesco with Dad.'

'Oh well, it's up to you. I'm going early. Tell him I've popped up west.'

'Why don't you tell him?'

'Because he won't let me go if I tell him.'

'Well maybe you shouldn't be going then.'

'Oh, Joni, you're such a goody two shoes.' I said and immediately wondered how and why I had come up with such an outdated phrase. 'I'm going and that's that. Enjoy your trip to Tesco.'

But she had gone, slamming the bathroom door behind her.

It was cold on the platform at six thirty the next morning. But I had to go before Dad woke up. So, I took the early train and arrived at Euston station about ten o'clock. There was a nice coffee shop open across the road, so I had some breakfast there and looked at my Jackie Summer Special. In small print at the bottom of the last page was the address of their offices. I double checked where I was going in the A-Z and made my way to the tube station. It was Thursday so it was busy with commuters, but I managed to get a seat next to a man with spread-eagled legs and a spread-eagled Telegraph. Since he was sharing his paper, I had a read of page four until he shook it violently and reined it in with a loud *tut*.

Outside the window opposite was just blackness because of the tunnel and I could see my reflection. My hair was messy, I hadn't had much time to get ready, and I hadn't put any make up on. I really did look like Mum I thought. And then I realised, it *was* Mum in the reflection, not me. The dark red lips, the blonde curls, the floral dress. I wasn't wearing a floral dress, so it couldn't be me. And then she smiled. She smiled at me with her ruby red lips. And I smiled back.

Hi darling, she said.

'Hi,' I replied. 'I didn't know you were coming with me.'

It was a last-minute decision.

'Oh, I'm glad. It's nice to have company.'

The man in the next seat looked at me out the corner of his eye, I could feel it. He folded his paper up into his brief case and stood up to get off at the next stop.

We're nearly there, Mum said.

'Oh yes,' I replied.

The tube went another two stops and we got off at Leicester Square. I walked up the escalator and when I got to the top, I realised I had lost Mum. She must have decided not to come with me after all, I thought. Oh well, not to worry.

I made my way through the busy streets, at some points there was hardly room to move on the pavement. Eventually I found the offices of Jackie magazine. Well, it was in a block with other offices. I went in through the revolving door and over to the reception desk. A young woman with wavy brown hair and big blue rimmed glasses sat behind the desk. She ignored me for a while, pretending she was busy with more important things and would get to me in her own good time. So I rang the bell on the desk which was right in front of her.

'Can I help you?' she asked not looking up.

'Yes, I'm here to see Cathy and Claire,' I said.

'Who?'

'Cathy and Claire, at Jackie magazine.'

'Do you have an appointment?' She was smiling sideways but still looking like she was doing something or other on her desk.

'No, but they know me, they'll see me.'

She picked up the phone.

'There's someone here for Cathy and Claire,' she continued smiling as she said it, and glanced up at me, and I realised it was a smirk on her face not a proper smile. I don't like smirks. Not at all. So, I leaned over the desk and grabbed a handful of her wavy hair. She screamed and dropped the phone.

'Stop smirking and get me Cathy and Claire,' I demanded.

Suddenly I was grabbed by two men in white shirts who held onto one arm each. I was pretty much lifted off my feet and there was a kerfuffle while they decided what to do with me.

'Take her into Mr. Bates' office,' someone shouted.

'I'll call the police,' said someone else.

So, I was transported to Mr. Bates' office to wait for the police. It was a small room, not really enough space in there for me and two burly security guards. They sat me on a chair and had to kneel one on either side of me to continue holding onto my arms.

'I won't pull anyone else's hair,' I said.

'We're not giving you the opportunity to run away,' one of them replied. So, we stayed in that position for a while. Then a man came in, who I presume was Mr. Bates and a woman with a beehive hairdo. The woman spoke first. 'We're just waiting for the police. Can you explain why you assaulted our receptionist?'

'She was smirking at me. I asked her to contact Cathy and Claire for me, and she smirked.'

The woman sucked in her cheeks, 'it's not acceptable to assault our staff, we will not tolerate it.' She turned to Mr. Bates.

'No, that's absolutely right,' he agreed. 'Can I ask why you needed to talk to er... Cathy and erm Claire?'

'My mum went missing on holiday, I wrote to them, and they never answered. I think they know what happened to her, I need to speak to them. They're hiding something, it's obvious.'

'I see,' said Mr. Bates and he turned and whispered something to the woman. 'Excuse us a moment.' Mr. Bates and the woman left the room.

The security guards and I continued to wait for a while. They were making huffing and puffing noises as their legs must have been extremely uncomfortable in the position they were in.

'I won't run away,' I said. 'Why don't you just guard the door?' They seemed to agree between themselves that this was a good idea and heaved themselves up just as the police arrived, a male and a female officer.

'It's okay fellas, you can leave it to us now,' said the male officer. They introduced themselves to me and I explained again the situation, about my mum and about Cathy and Claire.

'Well, I can understand it must have been a very difficult time for you,' said the male, 'but you can't go around grabbing people's hair because they smirk at you, otherwise we'd all be assaulting people.'

I hadn't thought of it that way, he did have a good point. Then the female officer spoke. 'I remember about your mum love, she wasn't found, was she?'

'No, she wasn't. But they know something, I'm sure.'

She nodded slowly. 'Okay,' she continued, 'well, I'll be honest, we are not going to pursue this, and the young lady you assaulted isn't going to press charges on this occasion. So, what we'll do, we'll give you a lift home today and have a word with your dad. Do you still live with your dad?'

'Yes, I do.' Inside I was curling over like a dried-up autumn leaf. The shame, the neighbours, Mrs. Thomas, Aunty Jean,

Dad. I was going to be the talk of the neighbourhood and not in a good way.

I left the building accompanied by the police like a common criminal. People in reception watched the sad spectacle, as did the woman with the wavy hair which I had grabbed. She actually gave me a little smile, not in a smirky way this time, but a proper smile, like she felt sorry for me or something.

Chapter 6

'What on earth were you thinking Billie?' Dad said after the police had finally left. 'Wait, don't tell me again, I know.' He sat down at the kitchen table opposite me. I chewed my lip. I couldn't make it any clearer, I'd explained why I did it. There was nothing more I could add.

Aunty Jean chipped in, 'you could have jeopardised your place at college. You have such a great opportunity there.' She leaned down towards me placing her arm across my shoulder, I stiffened. 'Don't ruin your chances love.'

'I don't intend to ruin my chances Jean,'

'*Aunty* Jean,' Dad interrupted.

'*Aunty* Jean. I don't intend to ruin my chances. But I needed to speak to them. That's all. About Mum.'

Dad sighed. 'You know there probably is no Cathy and Claire don't you love?'

'*What*?' I frowned, 'of course there is, they answer people's problems in Jackie magazine, it's a well-known fact. They've been doing it for years.'

'It's probably two middle-aged women called Jean and Maureen stuck in an office all day.' He turned to Aunty Jean raising his hand. 'No offence Jean.'

She raised an eyebrow and picked up a bowl off the table.

'The point is,' he continued, 'they don't know anything about Mum, they're just ordinary people doing a job.'

I said nothing. This conversation was going nowhere and now Dad was trying to throw in a curveball suggesting Cathy and Claire didn't even exist.

But I had to admit, Aunty Jean was right, as usual. I didn't want to risk losing my place at college. I had been so excited to be offered a place on the art foundation course. I had done very badly in my GCEs, but fortunately my art portfolio had convinced Mr. Mouseman, the head of the art school, that I might just have some potential as an artist. It gave me a boost to think I could actually, maybe, hopefully, make a career doing something I enjoyed, loved even.

'Okay, Aunty Jean, I'll admit I was silly to do what I did today and I'm glad it didn't ruin my chances at art school. I must have been overtired or something. I haven't been sleeping well lately.'

Aunty Jean looked up from ladling out soup. 'Haven't you Billie? Why didn't you say?'

Because you'd all think I've gone nuts if I told you, I thought. Night after night dreaming about Mum, swimming, diving, drowning. And if I wasn't dreaming about her, then I was listening to her, chatting on and on about this, that and the other, her life story, her childhood during the war, how she met Dad, her clinches with Frank. It was enough to keep anyone awake. But I just said: 'Oh, I don't know, I'm just over-excited about college I suppose.'

'Well, you must try and sleep, you've got a few weeks till college starts, you can't be not sleeping all the way till then.' Aunty Jean flashed me one of her sympathetic smiles which lasted around half a nano-second and handed me a bowl of soup.

'It's been an awfully long time hasn't it, Maggie? Since we saw mother.'

'Yes, it has Lizzie. Too bloody long. How is one feeling about it darling?'

The Queen sighed. 'A bit sort of- empty inside really, I'd say, yes, that's how I'd describe it. Time has gone by and it's all empty of Mum.'

I nodded and put my arm around the Queen, and we both took a long drag on our felt-pen ciggies. 'There's nothing to be done about it really is there? We just have to bloody well carry on Liz. What a piss-poor show.'

She started laughing, and so did I. 'Oh Maggie you're such a jolly old gal, what the bloody hell would one do without you?'

September came and Joni went back to school, college started a week later. I spent most of my time holed up in my room these days. Sometimes, Mum's chatter was so constant and demanding that I could hardly hear or concentrate on anything else. It was nice to have her back, but sometimes I wished she would go and bother someone else. She didn't though, at least, no one else seemed to be hearing her.

'Billie? Have you got a friend in there?' Dad asked.

'Sshh' I told Mum. 'No Dad.'

'Oh, I thought I heard you talking.'

'No Dad, it's just the radio.'

'Okay love. Are you coming down for dinner?'

'No, I'm not hungry.'

You must eat, said Mum. *You need to eat darling.*

'I know, but I'm just not hungry,' I said.

'Yes, alright love, I heard you. Let me know if you want anything.' I heard Dad's footsteps retreating down the stairs.

I buried my head in my hands, covering my ears, but it didn't help. She was still there.

Let's go out somewhere tomorrow, she said. *We could go to Camber River. The weather's still warm.*

'Alright, we can do that if you want.' I said, thinking it might be a good way to distract her, and give me a bit of peace.

65

So, the following morning I got up early, with Mum telling me what to do, what to wear, what to bring. I put my swimming costume on under my clothes, packed a towel, my purse and an egg and cress sandwich to eat on the bus. The journey took around forty minutes and all the time, she was chatting. *Look at the market square, ooh it's changed since I was a girl. Oh no where's Dillie's teashop gone?*

'It went ages ago Mum, they closed down, went bust.'

Went bust? Are you kidding? It was the best teashop in town!

I sighed, it was impossible, and people were looking sideways at me, I could feel eyes on me, pursed lips, whispers amongst the other passengers.

'Alright, everyone, have a good look.' I said loudly. And then I whispered to Mum, 'you have to be quiet; people are looking at us.'

What do I care? Let them stare, she laughed.

I sighed again and turned to look out the window.

When we got to Camber River there was no one else there. The day was warm, but it was cloudy, and the river was flowing fast after a weekend of rain.

Put the mat out then darling, Mum instructed. So I did. It was only nine thirty in the morning, but she insisted I should sunbathe. *You're too pale Billie, you need a bit of sunshine, a bit of vitamin D is good for your skin.* I lay on the mat for a while, even though the sun wasn't out. I kept my clothes on for now, feeling self-conscious in front of traffic going by on the nearby road.

66

You should have saved your sandwich, it would be nicer to have eaten it here, Mum said.

'You told me to eat it on the bus.'

If I told you to put your finger in the fire, would you?

'No of course not.'

Oh, I think you would darling, I think you'd do anything for me. Wouldn't you my love? Aww, come on Billie, I'm only joking. Let's go and look at the river from up on the bridge. Leave your stuff here.

We walked up and onto the bridge to look at the river, it was higher than it looked from down on the grass. I leaned over to see the swirling copper waters below. 'It's lovely isn't it?' I said, but Mum didn't answer. She didn't seem to be with me now. And then I saw her. Down in the river, wearing her flowery swimming cap, she waved and called to me. *Come in Billie, the water's lovely! Come on, oh darling, help, the river's taking me away, Help me Billie please!*

My eyes were wide, my breathing fast and broken. Mum was drowning, just like in my dreams. I didn't want to jump; it was so high, and the river was deep and flowing fast. But I had to save her, I couldn't lose her again. So, I climbed up onto the stone wall. And jumped.

Dear Cathy and Claire

I love my mum, but she is really getting on my nerves at the moment. I had an accident at the river because she went in the water even

67

though she can't swim. I don't know what to do, I want her to go
away, but she is my mum. I shouldn't feel like that, should I?
I'd be grateful for your advice if you have time.
Thank you
Billie Fisher

I was in A&E for a while, till they were sure I was okay physically. I had a few cuts and bruises and concussion, but I had been very lucky they said, it could have been much worse. The water was higher than usual, so that had been a blessing. But I was worried about Mum. Where was she? The doctor said that the medics and police did not see her at all and there had been no reports of anyone else in the river. Some people saw me jump apparently, and they said there was no one else there. I couldn't understand it. Mum must have managed to get out of the water by herself and then what? Had she just left me injured? So many questions and no way of answering them. I had to stop myself. I was concussed so of course I could not think straight. Later, when I felt better, everything would become clear, I reassured myself.

I was asked to wait for a little while in A&E and then I was seen by the psychiatric liaison nurse, she said her name was Georgie, and we had a short conversation about being girls with boy's names. She seemed quite young, about twenty-three I'd say, and she had blue hair and dark make up. She didn't wear a uniform, so I was a bit suspicious at first that she might not be a proper nurse, but she was very sympathetic, so I decided to trust her anyway. Georgie asked me a lot of questions. 'No, I didn't try to kill myself, I was trying to save my mother, she got into difficulties in the water.'

Georgie repeated what the A&E doctor had said, that Mum wasn't here now, and she hadn't been seen anywhere at the river. 'Well, she must be okay, she's probably waiting for me at home. Can I go now?' I said. Georgie asked if they could ring Dad because he was my next of kin. I wasn't happy about Dad knowing, it would just worry him. But she told me it was important, so I gave her our telephone number. Georgie asked me to wait then, till Dad came, and for the doctor to see me.

'But I've just seen a doctor,' I said.

'Ah yes I know, Billie. But another doctor wants to see you if that's ok. She is a doctor for mental health.'

'Oh, a psychiatrist you mean. I don't need a psychiatrist. I'm fine. Georgie, I'm fine, honestly. Why are you getting me a psychiatrist? I'm starting college next week. No, you're going to ruin it all for me.' I started to cry. Suddenly everything seemed to come crashing down on me, I couldn't control this stupid situation. *It was my life, who on earth did these people think they were, telling me I need to see a psychiatrist?*.

'Billie,' Georgie touched my arm, 'we just want to be sure that you are ok. You jumped from a bridge today, it could have been much more serious. We need to make sure you're safe. That's all. Doctor Khali is so nice, she will only want to help you.'

So, Dad and Doctor Khali turned up. Dad hugged me and cried, 'why, Billie, why would you jump off a bridge?' He sat next to me, then added, 'of course, it's all been too much hasn't it? Oh sweetheart, I'm sorry you've been suffering so much more than I realised.'

I wrinkled my nose, *suffering? I haven't been suffering. Have I?* Maybe I had but I didn't know it was called suffering.

Dr. Khali spoke, she had a very calm voice, all on one level, no ups and downs, nice and gentle, she made me feel safe like I could tell her anything and she wouldn't be surprised or shocked. Obviously, she was a very well-trained doctor. 'Billie, I would like you to come in and spend a few days on the ward so that we can help you. We'll try some medication which will alleviate your anxieties and help you to feel more able to cope with the difficulties and the worries you've been having.'

'Will it bring Mum back?' I asked a little sarcastically.

'No, it won't I'm afraid, but it might help you to deal with her loss. The nurses and the other staff will spend time with you so that you can talk about things, and they will offer what help they can.'

Well, it all sounded very nice, and I thought, maybe it would give me a chance to have a little rest before I start college, get my head together. If they're all like Georgie, then I wouldn't mind. As long as I'm out in time for college. 'Are you going to commit me?' I asked.

'Oh no, we try not to commit people these days,' said Dr Khali with a gentle smile. 'It's much better if people come in voluntarily for help. Of course, if someone is too ill to make that decision then doctors might want to bring the person into hospital. But you are agreeing to come in, so we will not have to think about any of that.'

I was glad; I didn't want to be committed like some loony off the street. Then I wondered, if I hadn't agreed, would they be bringing me in like some loony off the street? Oh God, maybe I *am* some loony off the street, I pushed that thought to the back of my mind.

The nurses on the ward weren't all like Georgie, unfortunately. Some were in the office all day and never came out. Some were running around like headless chickens, and some were constantly in meetings. I didn't know who was who, the charge nurses, the nursing assistants and the qualified nurses. They all dressed in their own clothes, so it was hard to tell them apart from each other and from the patients sometimes. Then I found a board on the wall with photos of the staff and their first names, so, after a few days I began to get a grip of who was who.

I had a named nurse called Phoebe. She was a bit older than Georgie, in her thirties perhaps. She was supposed to meet with me on a regular basis, but our *one-to-one time*, as she called it, seemed to become fewer and farther between. One minute she'd be on days, the next on nights, and then on sick leave for three months. Three months. These people were

71

supposed to be professional, but mostly they seemed as elusive as Cathy and Claire.

'What are you in for? If you don't mind me asking,' a young woman called Sandra asked over lunch one day. I say lunch, but that is being overly generous, it was slop really, mashed potato slop with some rubberised turkey meat and watery gravy. Anyway, I told her, I had jumped in the river to save my Mum who was drowning and had been admitted to hospital to rest and recover. 'Oh, gosh, that sounds awful,' Sandra said.

'Yes, it was. And also I keep getting fobbed off by Cathy and Claire, you know, the agony aunts in Jackie magazine.'

Sandra began to look a little puzzled.

'I wrote to them when my Mum disappeared a few years ago, but they never answered me. Now they are hiding what they know about where she went and what happened to her.'

'But she's back isn't she? So can't you just ask her?'

'She doesn't want to talk about it.'

'Oh, I see.'

I've noticed people seem to say *I see* a lot when I talk about Mum. But it's obvious that they don't see. They just don't know what else to say, I can't blame them, mine is a quite confusing story for someone who isn't directly involved. Sandra told me she had been brought into hospital because she'd taken an overdose. She and her named nurse had been talking about how she had had a very difficult upbringing and how she felt bad about herself. Someone must have made her feel like that, I don't know who. I liked Sandra, it seemed so unfair that she should spend her whole life disliking herself and harming herself. I wanted to help her, but it was hard to know how when I couldn't even help myself.

We both seemed to be locked into lives of trying to find answers and ways to rid ourselves of things we could not change. But we can never rid ourselves of what has happened. If only we can find a way to live with the bad thing, so that it becomes a part of us that we can put away, and only confront when we choose to. But of course, that is much, much easier said, than done.

I'd been here for four months, and I was feeling quite angry and upset about it. I had missed the start of college. Dad spoke to Mr. Mouseman and had my place deferred for a year. Nothing much seemed to be happening in hospital, every day was long and boring, punctuated only by a frustrated patient throwing their lunch tray across the dining room, or an exhausted nurse bursting into tears and running to the staff room. And they kept experimenting with my medication. Mum was a nuisance most of the time telling me not to trust the staff, not to take the tablets they were offering me. I didn't know what to do. I was taking the tablets for a long time, being *compliant*, as they said in handovers that I had heard through the door of the meeting room. But I was fed up. The drugs didn't seem to help me, I didn't feel better, I felt worse. They made me feel groggy and horrible so then I started refusing them, being *non-compliant* which Phoebe did not like at all. I think she thought it reflected badly on her nursing skills.

Dr. Khali, though, was very understanding, and she prescribed some different tablets which she thought might be better for me. Initially, I was willing to try them, but then Mum stuck her oar in. *You don't need them*, she said, *they think they know what they're doing but they don't.*

'Billie,' said Phoebe one day during a rare *one-to-one* session, 'you must take your medication. If you don't, you aren't going to get any better.'

'But Mum says I shouldn't take it and that you're all trying to poison me.'

'Billie, you know you're in hospital, don't you?'

'Of course I do. I'm not stupid. I'm here because I jumped off a bridge.'

'Mum told you to do that too, didn't she?'

'Yes, but she was drowning.'

'The thing is Billie; we think that these feelings are all part of your illness.

'It wasn't a *feeling*, it actually happened.' I interrupted, but Phoebe ignored my comment and carried on regardless.

'-And this new medication will help you to feel so much better, really Billie, it will. We want to help you, Billie, but you're making it very difficult for us when you won't take your tablets.' She looked at me with raised eyebrows, like someone addressing a puppy dog who has peed on the carpet. 'What do you say? Hmm?'

74

I wondered where Phoebe had trained to be a nurse, *The Andy Pandy School of Nursing* I decided.

'Okay, I will try it,' I said.

'Great,' she said, picking up her notes, 'I'll go and get it now.

Chapter 7

Mum was drunk by the sound of it. *You shouldn't have taken that shit*, she said. *Now look what you've done.*

'It's supposed to help me get better,' I told her.

Better? You're not even ill. For goodness' sake Billie, why are you trusting them? I'm your Mum, I want the best for you. They don't.

'Shut up Billie,' Sandra said, she was in the bed opposite me in the dorm. 'You're keeping us all awake. Tell your Mum to sling her hook.'

I buried my head under the blankets. I could hear Janet's radio in the next bed playing *Wham Bam I Am the Man*, but no one dared tell her to turn it down, including the staff.

The next day, we were all tired. I had been wild swimming with Mum all night, way up in the Scottish Highlands, I was freezing when I woke. A nurse came into the dorm, 'woo it's like Siberia in here,' she said going over to the window. It was open to its maximum three inches to prevent suicidal jumps or great escapes, but still, it was enough to let in plenty of freezing January air.

Dad and Joni came to visit me that day. We met in the family room as Joni was still under sixteen.

'Hey, we bought you a new nightie,' said Joni pulling out a cotton floral special from an M&S bag.

'Thanks,' I said, wondering what Janet would have to say about it. Dad gave me a kiss on the cheek. 'We're missing you at home sweetheart,' he said.

'*I'm* missing me at home,' I grinned ruefully. 'I'm taking my meds now so they should let me out soon.'

'There's a ward round on Thursday, I'll come to that,' Dad continued. 'You seem a bit better, do you feel any better love?'

I raised my eyebrows thoughtfully and breathed in. 'Er, yes, I think I do, thanks.'

'That's good then isn't it'? said Joni.

'Oh yes Lizzie, it's jolly good,' I joked. 'And how is one?'

She laughed; Dad looked puzzled. 'Fan-bloody-tastic,' she said. 'I've got tickets to go and see *Shakin' Stevens* next week with my friend Gill.'

'Oh, my goodness,' I raised my eyebrows. 'You lucky thing.'

Our conversation went on like that. It was good to see them, and to be honest, I was feeling a little more like myself. Though it's hard to know who *myself* really was. My pre-twelve-year-old self sounds a bit weird, but that was my best time, my pre-mum-disappearing days. Ever since, I have not been myself. Perhaps I needed to forge a new *myself* because I didn't really like being the self who jumped off a bridge.

On Thursday, we all trooped into ward-round after hanging around all morning waiting for Dr. Khali, who had been unavoidably held up by an emergency. A junior doctor, Dad, Phoebe, a student nurse, an OT and a psychologist who I had never seen before in my life, all gathered in the meeting room, to discuss my 'progress on the ward,' as Phoebe put it in her introduction. Dr. Khali asked me if I was still hearing Mum's voice and I told her I did sometimes, but she was much fainter now and slurred, like she was drunk. She asked me if I still felt compelled to do what Mum told me to do. I said no, and that she didn't really tell me to do things anymore. Phoebe chipped in at this point and said that I didn't seem to be talking to myself as much as I had before. 'Responding,' she called it,

77

'not responding' as much. Everyone smiled and nodded, and Phoebe made a few notes for my records.

Then Dr. Khali gave me a very gentle lecture about keeping on with my medication and I would be able to go home and see how it went.

'Home, when?' I asked.

'Well do you think you will be able to continue with your medication there?' Dr. Khali asked.

'Yes, of course.' *Anything for you*, I thought. 'I will keep up with it,' I looked at Dad. He smiled and added, 'I'll make sure she takes it, Dr. Khali.'

'Good, well tomorrow then,' she said, just like that. Tomorrow. I could have jumped up and kissed her, but I didn't. I held my nerve. 'Thank you, thank you so much.'

'Alright, Billie, but you must come back next week to ward-round, and we'll see how you're getting on. And I'm going to arrange for you to see a specialist nurse for some talking therapy. Will you meet with her for me?'

'Yes, I will.' I was as agreeable as a kitten, as long as I was going from this God-forsaken place, I would do anything dear Dr. Khali asked of me.

The next day, I said goodbye to the other patients, and we wished each other luck. I gave Sandra a big hug and told her to look after herself and that I hoped I would see her again. Dad and Aunty Jean picked me up, Joni was in school, but we were going to pick her up on the way home. Home, I couldn't believe I was going there at last. Aunty Jean hugged me like

78

she'd never hugged me before and Dad carried my bag to the car. When we arrived home with Joni, she said, 'come up to your room, come on.' When I went into my old room, I hardly recognised it. 'We've all helped do it, even Aunty Jean,' Joni said. They all stood in the doorway with hopeful expressions.

The walls were papered with a green and yellow patterned paper, a bit jungle-like with toucans hiding among palm leaves. The wall behind my bed was plain yellow with a huge poster of Fleetwood Mac on it because they were my new thing, out with Donny and boy bands, it was Fleetwood Mac for me now. Joni pressed a button on the tape recorder and *'Welcome Home'* by Peters and Lee started playing. I laughed even though my eyes were full of tears, and I sat on my new green bedspread. 'It's really beautiful, I love it, thank you all so much.' We all had a big group hug and cried a lot. Dad had to lend everyone his hankie, we weren't bothered about germs, we were all just so glad that I was home.

'What was your mum like Billie?' Asked Lorea, the Spanish *Specialist Nurse*. 'How do you remember her?'

I cast my mind back six years. I see Mum as she walks away from me at Newell Hall when I first went up to the house to ride Bay. Her pink print dress and her blonde curls are blowing in the breeze and she's looking back at me, blowing me a kiss with her matt red lips. And she smiles that big, bright, beautiful smile.

My eyes began to prickle. 'She had blonde curly hair, and red lips. Always red lips. She was beautiful.'

'She sounds lovely.'

'She did everything for us, always looking after everyone.'

'What was her name?'

'Edith Nina Baker, but she hated Edith, she always called herself Nina.'

Lorea smiled and nodded. 'A good name. What kind of things did she do for you?'

'She sewed. Always making dresses on her machine for me and my sister. She took us to the market to choose fabrics and lace.' I smiled at the memory. 'It was always sunny. I remember my childhood, always being sunny.' I laughed, 'but it couldn't have been could it? It must have rained sometimes.'

'Perhaps it seems sunny because it was a happy childhood.'

'Yes, it was happy. I was happy.'

Lorea made a few notes. 'When your mother speaks to you now, do you think she is the same person you've just described? Does she still make you happy.'

I swallowed and thought. 'She's not always kind, no.' I bit my lip. 'It doesn't seem like the same person, but who else could it be?'

'You. Billie. It could be you, your own mind, searching for her. Or perhaps you're punishing yourself.'

'Why would I punish myself?'

'Billie, I'm not saying you are. I'm just trying to explore things with you. Your mother loved you didn't she?'

'Yes.' I blubbed.

'She would never have hurt you?'

'No.'

'Do you think you hurt her in some way?'

'Yes.'

'How do you think you hurt her; can you tell me?'

'I wasn't there when she needed me. I never said goodbye.' And my eyes overflowed and flowed rushing tears down my hot, red cheeks. 'I left her on her own. I can't forget it.'

'You don't have to forget it Billie. But your lovely mum, she wouldn't have wanted her little girl to punish herself for the rest of her life would she? Do you think she would want you to forgive yourself? Do you think she might say *there's nothing to forgive?*'

'Yes, she would.' I nodded wearily and wiped my eyes. Lorea had laid her hand on mine. She looked a bit teary too. It must be a very emotional job being a specialist nurse and listening to everyone's tragedies, I thought.

Dad and I went back to the hospital the following Thursday for ward round. Dr. Khali was pleased to hear that my week at home had gone well. 'What did you do?' she asked.

'Went to Tesco. Read a bit. Er- that's about it,' I said.

'You met up with Cheryl,' Dad reminded me.

'Oh yes, I met up with Cheryl.'

Phoebe wrote that down.

'Well, that all sounds great, Billie. I'm glad you took things easy. I think you've done really well. And you took all your meds?'

'Yup, I did.'

81

'Good. Well I think we can be looking at discharging you soon. Have another week at home and then, if it goes well again we'll discharge you next week. But keep up your sessions with Lorea alright? Is that all ok?'

It was all ok with me. I was just pleased to be going home and looking forward to being discharged. And I liked Lorea, she was helping me a lot with thinking about Mum and getting things into perspective.

Dad and I stopped off at Wimpy for lunch to celebrate.

'I'm very proud of you,' he said as he sat down with the tray of burgers and fries and coke. 'You're a real gem.'

'A gem?' I laughed.

'Yes, Billie, a gem. A precious stone.'

A gemstone. Blue and speckled with copper like the one Joni had threaded to make a necklace for Mum. Where was that necklace now? Whether she was alive or dead, it might still be there, around Mum's neck. The thought chilled me to the bone.

'You've gone pale Billie, are you okay, love?'

I took a deep breath, 'I'm okay Dad, thanks.'

We ate our burgers and fries and drank our coke and agreed that I had come a long way recovering from a breakdown like that. But my thoughts were distracted by the gem. The duck-egg blue stone resting against Mum's smooth, pale skin.

I was walking past Bunnies Café one sunny day in April. I had just turned eighteen and was looking forward to starting college in the autumn. Dr. Khali had discharged me from the hospital although I still went in for outpatients' appointments

82

and to see Lorea. In fact, that was where I had just been when I passed Bunnies and decided to pop in for a coffee. I was on my own, but I didn't care. The mood I was in, I could do anything I liked.

As I opened the door to go in I noticed a sign on the window:

Waitress/Waiter Wanted

It got me thinking. I could do with a little job/cash/independence. So I went inside, still thinking about the notice. The cafe was busy, steamy and noisy and I found a table near the back. I rested my elbow on the table and my chin in my hand, still contemplating the idea of having a job at Bunnies. A waitress came over, she was about my age, with red hair in a messy bun, black t-shirt and skirt, and a little apron. She looked frazzled, but she was earning money. She was making her own way in the world, able to pay for the cinema or a new bag when she wanted to, without having to ask her dad.

'Is the job still vacant?' I asked her.

'Oh, yeah I think so,' she replied. 'I'll get Maddie, she's the manager.'

'Ok, thanks, and can I have a coffee and cheese on toast please?'

I had finished my lunch and the café had quietened down when Maddie the manager came over. 'Hi,' she said, 'were you interested in the job?'

I told her I was, and she sat down at my table. After some gruelling questions which I answered with fair dollop of imagination, she gave me the job. Twenty hours a week, most of them at the weekend for no extra pay, but I was thrilled to bits at my first job interview success. I rushed home to tell everyone.

'Remember what Dr. Khali said about stress,' Dad warned me.

'Oh I know, I know, but it's stressful not having money at my age, I should have a little job. I need to buy stuff, go places. I can't live on the breadline forever.'

Dad conceded and I agreed that if it became too much for me, I would give it up.

I dreamt I was sitting alone by a beautiful lake, the blue-green waters lapping gently against the shingle shore. Tall pines lined the edge of the water and high above me, buzzards flew, crying to each other and hovering against the darkening sky. From the deep waters rose a hand, reaching upward like the *Lady of the Lake* in Arthurian legend. And the hand was holding Joni's pendant, the smooth blue stone with copper flecks, its golden thread wrapped between long, pale fingers. That's all. That was my dream. I woke up and wrestled with the emotions this scene had evoked. Bewilderment, sadness, fear.

'I'm no expert on dreams,' said Lorea, 'but clearly something has brought back a memory of the pendant, perhaps it was to do with what your dad said the other day at the burger place.'

I agreed with this, yes it was that word- *gem*, it had triggered the memory of the stone pendant. But it was the context of the dream that made me feel so uneasy, as if I knew something, but could not remember. Why water all the time? Why was Mum always swimming, or drowning, or calling me to rescue her from water? It was a recurring theme. Lorea did not have the answers, but I appreciated her help, at least she was trying, not like Cathy and Claire.

I started work at Bunnies the following Saturday. Maddie said I was going to be in the kitchen, washing up, for most of the time, but she would teach me to make the coffees this week and maybe serve one or two customers. Then, when I had mastered the washing up and the coffee, I would be trained properly to work *front of house*, as she called it. Even though it was a small café, working *front of house* would be the epitome of my waitressing career I felt, something that would look very good on my CV if the art didn't work out.

I arrived in good time, eight-twenty, wearing my black v-neck top and a knee length skirt that Aunty Jean had helped me pick out at Hennes. I felt the bee's knees, a working girl, like Sandra off *The Liver Birds*. But I was nervous too I must admit and on entering Bunnies I had an urge to turn round and run straight home. But I didn't. Maddie was in the tiny kitchen with the chef. He was frying some sausages and she was whisking up some eggs. 'Hi Billie, put your jacket on the hook there,' she said, pointing to hooks on the kitchen door. 'This is Pete, our chef, and that's Tania.' Maddie pointed over to the waitress I had spoken to when I first enquired about the job, she was wiping a table and, on hearing her name, she looked up, waved at me and smiled.

We set up the café before opening at nine, filling the salt and pepper pots and pouring cheap ketchup into good quality ketchup bottles. We took cupcakes and soup out of the freezer to defrost in time for lunch. And then we opened the doors. There was no one waiting to come in, but eventually a customer arrived at ten o'clock. He was an elderly man with greying hair and liver spots on his forehead. 'Hello dear, are you new?' he said to me as I showed him to a table.

'Yes, I am, my name is Billie.'

'Ahh, Billie Holiday, I usually sit by the window, do you mind?'

'Of course not,' I said, and let him pick his own table. 'I was named after Billie Holiday actually.'

'Aha! I knew it,' the old man laughed, 'no one else could sing quite like her.'

'No, they definitely couldn't,' I agreed.

'Maddie!' the old man called, 'got any Billie Holiday on the sound system?'

'Oh, no, please, not on my account,' I said, I wasn't at all sure about this. It was a long time since I had heard Billie singing, even though she was my namesake. But too late, Maddie called back, 'I have, Lenny!' Here it is, I'll put the tape on now.'

And then, came Billie's sweet, wavering voice filling the café at ten o'clock in the morning with *That Ole Devil Called Love*. Oh, gosh, I don't know how I held myself together, but I did. I did. I remembered Mum as I watched Maddie pouring the coffee and as I took Lenny his Eggs Benedict. And I wondered what she'd think of her little girl now, serving customers in a café, washing dishes in an industrial sink. She would be proud of me, I knew it. So I didn't cry or fall apart as Billie was singing, even though she reminded me of swaying in the kitchen with Mum. I just washed the dishes and smiled a little smile to myself, my new improved, growing-up-lovely self.

Chapter 8

I spent much of my time working at Bunnies through the rest of August. I made the most of the hours I could pick up because I knew once college started, I would only be able to work weekends. The cafe was very busy through the summer, and sometimes, Maddie would call me in unexpectedly because she was short of staff. But I didn't mind, it kept me from brooding about Mum. And I enjoyed being part of the little café community, staff and customers. The Bunnies crowd.

Lenny was a regular, and Fred too, there seemed to be a few older men, widowers, who came to Bunnies for a little social contact in an otherwise lonely day. Or so I supposed, that's how it seemed anyway.

'Ooh you're a good girl,' said Fred as I put down his coffee and cream in front of him one morning. 'What a beauty,' he winked, 'and the coffee's not bad either.'

I rolled my eyes and returned behind the counter. Maddie was away that day, so there was only me, Pete, Tania and another waiter Graham. He was new, only seventeen, quiet and a bit wet behind the ears.

'I think he's got his eye on you,' Tania whispered to me in the kitchen. Pete turned, smiled and winked, 'definitely,' he said.

'Oh stop it, he has not,' I said, 'you two are just trying to cause trouble.'

'Nooo really, I keep seeing him looking at you out the corner of his eye,' said Tania.

'He's just looking and learning from the expert,' I joked. But now they'd made me think about wet-behind-the-ears Graham, and the thought that he might have *his eye on me* made me a little self-conscious. But time went by, and he never made a move, thank God. Perhaps he was shy, or perhaps my *don't come near me* vibes kept him at bay. I know I had a tendency to do that. I wasn't really up for romance or whatever you call it, a relationship or just a casual thing. I still had too much going on in my head and I didn't want to add to it with the complexities of love or lust or whatever. Oh not crazy stuff, I don't think I was relapsing or anything. But Mum was still there, somewhere, in the back of my mind, like she was on stand-by, or muted by the medication. I could feel her hovering in the background, not my real mum, but my version of her, the one who wanted to punish me. I still felt responsible in some way. Despite Lorea's best efforts, I couldn't quite shake off that feeling. I dreaded she might come back, and that I would lose my *insight*, as Dr. Khali called it. I feared I might slip back into that world where I believed everything that crazy version of Mum said to me.

September came and it was time to go to college. The beginning of a new chapter in my life; now was my chance to finally grow up and work for the career that I wanted, and I couldn't wait to get started. I missed the bus on the first day and got to college half an hour late for the first *Welcome* lecture. The lecture theatre was bursting at the seams with new talent all watching intently as Mr. Mouseman gave the inaugural address. The room turned as one to see me enter the theatre- stage left, my hair bathed in sweat from running up the hill to college. It was a mortifying start to my artistic career. *But,* I thought as I took the nearest empty space next to a slightly greying mature student, *I will laugh about it one day on 'Desert Island Discs.'*

The greying mature student shoved up along the bench-seat a little and smiled reassuringly at me, whispering, 'never mind, things can only get better.' We had a lot of forms to fill in. I took a sneaky glance at my mature neighbour's date of birth, 03/07/1942. *Forty years old, oh my God, he was born during the war!* I had to admire him for his fortitude, starting a new career at that age.

Once all the form filling was completed we had a chance to meet and greet each other, drink tea or coke in the main entrance hall and have a little tour around the different art departments. It was an easy day all in all, no work, just chatting, snacking and touring. We were divided into groups and, for the first few months and would all have a go at everything. Then we would get a chance to specialise in the area that rocked our boats the most. My plan was illustration, but who knows? The plan might change if I found another speciality I preferred, I decided I would keep my options open.

There were nine in our group. Two mature students, the man who I had been sitting next to in the lecture theatre, who's name, I found out, was Greg; and a woman who seemed a bit younger than him, called Marnie, like the Hitchcock character, well she probably wasn't like the *character*, I hoped not anyway. Turned out she was the great granddaughter of one of the original suffragettes, and this was a great talking point at lunchtime. Also in my group was a girl called Gill, two lads who were already friends, Steve and Dan, and then there was Mike, Helen and Alice. They seemed a nice crowd, sociable and friendly. During the afternoon, our groups were shown the rooms where we would be based. Ours was on the ground floor, a big airy room, it smelt of the paint and white spirit of generations which had seeped into the very fabric of the building. Because the building had originally been a church, the room had huge arched windows letting in lots of autumn sunshine. 'Wow, nice,' commented Alice, 'I like this very much, it has a great vibe.' We all agreed that it did have a great vibe.

Eric, our tutor, was a seasoned artist by the look of him, and a seasoned smoker and drinker I soon learned. I got the impression he was a pretty easy-going kind of person who took a very laid-back approach to teaching. Our first group seminar was held at a local pub- *The Craic*. 'Hopefully, you'll enjoy the course, and get a lot out of it,' Eric said in his gravelly thirty-a-day-voice, 'but if you don't, it's your own fault,' and with that forthright comment he guffawed with laughter and downed three whiskies in a row. I was pretty impressed.

I was happy going home that afternoon, looking forward to the following day when we would be starting with some silk-screen printing. Alice had joked that she would be making herself a groovy headscarf. But it turned out it wasn't printing on silk; it was printing with a silk-screen onto paper. 'The clue is in the name,' Eric commented as we all trundled off to the Kahlo building for a day of printing. I enjoyed our first proper day of the course. We had fun as a group, creating and making, like being at primary again, but for grown-ups. And afterwards we all went to the pub for further group bonding.

'How's university?' asked Aunty Jean one day. I was about two months into my course, and we were having tea at home one Friday evening. Jean had come round to cook for Joni and me, one of her specialities: spaghetti bolognese with garlic bread.

'It's not university,' I replied. 'I'm not that clever, it's college and it's going great thanks Jean, I love it.'

'*Aunty* Jean,' Joni corrected me whilst stuffing garlic bread into her mouth.

'Well, you certainly *are* clever enough for university,' Aunty Jean continued, 'but as long as you're enjoying the college, that's the main thing.'

I sighed, but as usual, I forgave her thoughtless comment because of her soldier boyfriend.

After we had finished dinner and were just sitting down to watch Aunty Jean's favourite telly programme, *Are You Being Served*, Dad arrived home from work. He was much later than usual, and he wasn't alone. Accompanying him into the lounge was a medium-sized, scruffy, supposed-to-be-white dog called Freddy. He looked like Tin Tin's dog, Snowy but greyer. He immediately peed on the carpet, but Joni and I had already fallen in love with him the minute he walked through the door.

'He belonged to Pat's daughter,' Dad told us. 'But she's split up with her other-half and she's having to move into a flat. The dog is only a year old, it's a shame. I felt sorry for him I must admit. I thought, perhaps we could give him a nice home.'

Pat was one of Dad's colleagues at work, the admin lady. 'She told me about him last week,' he continued. 'I said we'd take him, I thought it'd be nice for you girls to have a little dog.'

'Oh, he's so cute,' Joni stroked Freddy's head as he licked some peanut butter off her hand. Aunty Jean's expression said: *don't ever ask me to look after that creature*, she didn't actually say it, but her face did. She went and got her coat to go home. We thanked her for tea, but we were too entranced with our new arrival to see her to the door. 'I'll give you a lift,' Dad said, but she was already halfway up the path.

'How can we have a dog though, Dad?' I asked, 'I'm working or at college, you're at work and Joni's at school.'

'I know Bill, but I knew you'd love him, and I thought we can work something out. Perhaps one of us, probably you, Billie, or me, can take him out early in the morning, then Joni can take him out at three when she gets home from school.'

93

I thought about this, and then my brain started ticking over, as it does sometimes, coming up with a little plan. 'Hmm, I bet I could take him to college with me sometimes. When we're sitting around painting or just mooching around college, it wouldn't make any difference to anyone else if I had him with me.'

'Yes, we can work something out, he won't be alone for long,' Joni said hopefully. We weren't sure about the dog's name, Freddy, it reminded us of a chocolate frog. So we renamed him *Teddy*. He seemed to like it, jumping around all over the place when we called him. We offered him little treats of cheese when he came to us at the call of his new name, and it seemed to do the trick.

It turned out Pat's daughter and her ex had not done much training with Teddy. That weekend, we all paid the price. He was up whining and crying most of the night, weeing everywhere and wanting company. Luckily, we didn't have to get up early the next day, or the day after. And he was so adorable, that we couldn't be cross or impatient with him. Joni and I spent Friday and Saturday night cuddling and playing with him and taking him outside, rewarding him for doing his business in the garden. After a couple of weeks, he was like a changed dog, house-trained (almost) with a lovely white fluffy coat after a good wash and brush up. Even Aunty Jean gave him a little pat on occasion and looked as if she was warming to our new baby.

I asked at college if I could bring Teddy in with me sometimes, and Eric wasn't bothered at all. 'As long as the group don't mind,' he said. And they didn't. So Teddy became a regular visitor to college, following close on my heels wherever I went and lying patiently when I was busy printing or drawing. Soon everybody knew and loved Teddy. He came to my lectures and to The Craic after college, and I was careful not to drink too many *Loco Lobos* as I had a dependent to take care of. I loved having Teddy with me, he was my faithful little companion, my shadow, my best friend.

I was working one Sunday afternoon in Bunnies when I saw a familiar face. I had some difficulty placing the face, it was pretty enough, but with sunken cheeks from smoking and worrying and it belonged to a woman, aged about thirty with light brown straight hair, brown eyes, glasses and narrow, chewed lips, and then it came to me. It was Sandra, from the hospital. I went over to take her order and said, 'hi, do you remember me?'

'Oh God, Billie, *named-after-Billie-Holiday*,' she laughed, 'of course I remember you! How are you?' Sandra seemed really pleased to see me, and I was pleased to see her too. But then, I felt a bit worried that the other staff might hear us talking and realise that I'd been in a mental hospital.

'I'm fine,' I said quietly. 'How are you?'

'Oh I'm ok yeah, I'm out on a week's leave, staying with my mother. She's just in the loo.' At that moment, her mother returned from the loo, and Sandra introduced us. 'This is

95

Billie, I met her at Freshwood Hospital.' I nearly died. She said it with her voice at normal volume, and I was sure the whole café must have heard. Everyone must have known that Freshwood was the mental hospital on the outskirts of town. As kids we made jokes about it, the way kids do, *'you'll end up in Freshwood,'* that kind of thing. I wished the floor would open and swallow me up. Sandra's mum then added to my torment by saying, 'you certainly need to have a friend in that place, how nice that you two had each other. Are you better now dear?'

'Yes thanks,' I squeaked. 'Are you ready to order?'

They had full English breakfasts and I spent most of the next hour in the toilet or the store cupboard. I felt sure everyone must now know I had a mental illness, and I was mortified. I couldn't face them anymore.

After Sandra and her mother left, I came out of the store cupboard. Everything was quiet. Pete and Tania were cleaning up in the kitchen, Maddie was counting out the day's takings, 'Oh there you are Billie,' she said without looking up. Graham was wiping Lenny's table, hinting that he needed to hurry up with his coffee. But Lenny, oblivious to the fact that it was closing time, continued reading the paper. Gerry Rafferty was singing *Baker Street* on the cassette player for the umpteenth time that day. No one seemed perturbed in any way. I picked up some cups off an empty table and took them to the kitchen. Tania smiled at me, 'ok?' she said.

'Er yes thanks, are you?' I replied. She didn't answer, just nodded. *Does she know?* I thought, *why did she ask if I'm ok?*

I went home feeling very unsettled about the afternoon's incident, Sandra coming in and all the talk about Freshwood. I was so worried that Maddie had heard, that everyone had heard, well, Lenny wouldn't have because he was hard of hearing, so that was some comfort. But the others would have, and Maddie, what must she think of me? She was probably annoyed that I didn't mention my mental illness at the interview, even though it was a very impromptu interview. Over dinner that evening, I was brooding over my fish pie, thinking, *she's probably getting my P45 ready right now*, when Dad said, 'what's up Bill? You look lost in thought, was work ok?'

'Nothing, it was fine, I'm ok, just thinking about college tomorrow.' Then I had another worrying thought. Was I supposed to declare my illness to the college? What if they find out and kick me off the course? My head was swirling when I went upstairs to my room. I hadn't even thought about all this till now, that I might be supposed to tell people I'd been in Freshwood hospital. They'd want to know who they were employing/teaching surely. The more I thought about it, the more I convinced myself that I was committing some kind of unlawful fraud or deception punishable by a long prison sentence.

Chapter 9

I hadn't dreamt about Mum for a couple of months, but now, the dreams returned with a vengeance. Always in water, always swimming, then the next minute, screaming for help and eventually drowning. I would wake in a cold sweat and feel tired and unsettled for the rest of the day. Then one night in my dream, she spoke to me. I saw her blue eyes looking into mine and her red lips mouthing the words: *Stop taking those tablets, Billie, everyone will find out you're taking medication, if you stop, they'll know you're better.* Why should I listen to her? I asked myself when I woke. I knew I shouldn't listen, but she was so convincing, so real. Dad had given me responsibility for taking my tablets, he knew I had insight and that I knew the importance of taking them. I felt bad deceiving him, but I couldn't seem to help myself. I stopped taking them, I took two out of the packet each day and flushed them down the loo.

After a week without medication, I was surprised at how great I felt. I was going to work and college and getting on with everything without worrying that people might know I'd been mentally ill, I wasn't on any medication so how could they know? And when Mum said to me one day, *Billie, you're so much nicer now you're not on those tablets,* I knew I'd done the right thing.

In college we were up to starting on our chosen pathway. I was choosing illustration because it's what I'd always wanted to do, and though I had tried other areas of art, like animation, photography and graphics, I decided to stay with illustration. So our little group was splitting up, we'd still all be in the same building, but I would be in the illustration room, and they would be in their chosen specialist rooms. Three others from our group were doing illustration too- Greg and Marnie the mature students, Alice and myself.

'I've loved drawing since I could first pick up a pencil,' Greg said, sketching the outlines of a seaside town scene. 'It's in my blood.' Greg was on the drawing board next to mine in our new first floor art room.

'Really?' I replied, 'mine too. I mean, it's in my blood too,' I said. He laughed. I squinted over at his work. 'That's nice, it reminds me of somewhere I've been.' My mind drifted back to Seahouses with its bustling streets and fresh, salty sea air. I could almost taste the fish and chips and candy floss.

'Does it?' Greg said, 'I'm doing it from memory, it's a little place I went many years ago in Ireland.'

'Ireland? Oh, it reminds me of Seahouses in Northumberland.'
'Ah, these little fishing villages, they're all much of a muchness,' he joked.
You should go back there for a little holiday, Mum said.
'I'm not sure I'd want to do that,' I replied.
'Sorry?' Greg turned to me with a puzzled expression.
'Oh, I was just thinking, sorry. Thinking out loud.'
'Ahh, first sign of madness,' he smiled turning back to his picture. I was silent, *he knows*, I thought. Then Greg looked back to me, as if he'd read my mind and realised that he had said the wrong thing. It must have been obvious from my face that I was anxious and un-nerved because he asked, 'are you ok Billie? I was only joking you know.'
'Yes, yes, I'm fine, oh I know you were. I'm fine, just going to get some yellow ochre.' And I went off in search of yellow ochre that I didn't even need.

I liked the new art room, it was bright and sunny like the last room, but smaller, cosier somehow. It had the familiar smell of paint, white spirit and cigarette smoke ingrained into the well-worn drawing boards and the paint-stained wood floors. There were seven of us altogether now. The four from our original group were joined by Rob, Valerie and June. We all hit it off straight away. It was such a nice way to spend the day, drawing and painting together, listening to Scritti Politti on a loop. And I had little Teddy sleeping at my feet or running along to *Buckland's Bar* with us for breaks.

When I wasn't at college I was usually working at Bunnies, my time seemed to be completely full, with very little left to think about anything else but art and waiting on tables. I began to feel very tired. One Saturday I woke to get ready for work, which started at eight-thirty, I was just getting out of bed, when Mum said, *just don't go, they can manage, give yourself a day off Billie, you deserve it.*

'I can't do that Mum, I'm on the rota for today.' But the idea was very tempting, would they miss me? I was sure they could manage without me. So I got back into bed and lay there listening to Mum. *That's it, sod them, let them do the work, they hate you anyway, they prefer it when you're not there.*

Did they prefer it when I wasn't there? Probably. I was a bit useless really, I was a mental case. Who'd want me working in their café? I drifted back off into a restless sleep.

'Bill- Billie, wake up love,' Dad was knocking on my door. 'Maddie's on the phone, you're supposed to be in work.' He pushed the door open a little. 'It's ten o'clock, love. Aren't you well?'

'Yes, I'm well,' I whispered from under the duvet. 'I don't need to go in. I'm too tired.'

Dad came into the room and sat on the bed; I felt the mattress dip under his weight. 'Billie,' he said.

'What?'

'Billie, look at me please.'

I pushed the duvet down off my face. 'What?'

'Why didn't you go to work?'

101

You don't have to answer him, you know, said Mum.

'Oh shut up,' I said.

'Billie, please don't speak to me like that.'

'I'm sorry Dad, I wasn't speaking to you.'

'I see, well who were you speaking to?'

'No one. I was just thinking.'

'Okay, Bill, I'm going to tell Maddie that you're not well, that you overslept because you're not well, I'll apologise to her. Don't worry.'

So I had the day off, lying in bed, worrying and listening to Mum's incessant voice. And then a very odd and disconcerting thing happened. Mr. Newell arrived. *'Hello dear,'* he said in his posh northern tone.

'Hello, how did you get here?' I asked.

'By train of course, did you think I flew? Like One Flew Over the Cuckoo's Nest?' He and Mum laughed like a pair of hyenas as if it was the funniest thing anyone ever said.

Things were quiet the next couple of days, I slept a lot, it was my escape from the two voices that were tormenting me. But in sleep, I had my dreams to contend with. Dad popped his head round the door a few times, and once or twice he sat on my bed and started asking questions about my tablets. I told him to go away, I was eighteen, nearly nineteen now, it was none of his business. Apparently I had an appointment with Lorea at four o'clock on Tuesday, I told Dad I wasn't going, I was better now, I didn't need her anymore.

I think it must have been Wednesday when I realised that half of Freshwood hospital was in my bedroom. Dr. Khali, some social worker called Guy, Lorea and Dad. All crowding in. It was nice of them to visit, but, I assured them, I was alright and just needed some more sleep. Dr. Khali's voice, gentle as summer raindrops, filled the room, 'Billie, we're all worried about you, you've missed a week at college and work. Now that's not a problem in itself, but it does tell me that something is wrong. Dad says you're not taking your tablets. And we are worried that Mum's voice has come back and is upsetting you. I really want to help you Billie, I know your college course means a lot to you.'

There was a lot to think about there. I needed to *unpick* what she'd said. *Unpick* was a Phoebe word, it was a good word, except when she said it, in that patronising way of hers. So I began to unpick what Dr. Khali had said.

'First of all I haven't missed a week, only two days because I was tired. Also, what does Dad know about my tablets? I was taking them, and then- okay, I stopped because Mum told me to. And third, or fourth- or whatever- it's two voices not one. And, also, you don't need to worry, I'm not upset, I'm fine. Honestly. Thanks for coming, but I'm fine.' I put my head under the duvet again. *That's my girl,* said Mum.

'Two voices? Do you know who the other one is?'

'Mr. Newell.'

I heard a sigh; I think it was Dad. Then there was some mumbling and people going out of the room. I felt a weight on the bed, and Dr. Khali's voice spoke again. 'Billie, I'd like you to come back into hospital, just for a few days while we sort your medication out.'

'No, absolutely not.' I threw the duvet back off my face. 'Last time I was in for months on end. No way. I've got too much to do. It'll end my career before it's even started; I have to finish my course.'

'Billie, I need you to come in with me now. Please, I want to help you get well again. You were doing really well.'

'And if I don't?'

'Well…'

'You will drag me in just because you can and ruin my whole life?'

'I don't want to force you to come in, Billie, I don't think we need to go down that route, I think you know deep down that you need help. I only want you to stay a very short time while we help you with your medication.'

Help me with my medication, as if it was something I wanted, like help with make-up tips or something. As if I liked having medication to dull my senses and my life. As if I had a choice. So back I went to Freshwood, for another indeterminate length of time, no doubt destroying any chance I had for a career in art. Despite her gently persuasive bedside manner and my admiration for Dr. Khali, I felt inwardly quite angry with her.

Sandra was back on the ward when I arrived, sitting in the lounge area with a few other patients. 'Hi Billie,' she said, 'I only just saw you working in Bunnies, what happened? I thought you were doing so well.'

'So did I,' I replied, 'but suddenly everything came crashing down around my ears, I don't know what happened really.' I shrugged and flashed her a brief smile of resignation.

'I'm sorry to hear that Billie.'

'Thanks, how did your leave go?'

'It went alright, thanks, Mum was getting me down though, she's not the most upbeat sort of person, she made me feel like I actually *wanted* to come back to hospital.'

'Oh no, I'm sorry, Sandra. What's the plan then? Is there a new plan?'

'I'm not sure,' she took off her glasses and wiped them on her T-shirt. 'I've got ward round tomorrow, we'll talk about it then, but I'm worried about telling Mum that I don't want to live with her anymore.'

'I can see that would be very difficult,' I agreed. 'But you've got to do what's best for you Sandra. It's your health, your life.' I don't know where I got such a pearl of wisdom from, but I thought, I ought to be following that advice myself.

Dad let Mr. Mouseman know that I was ill again. He told him I was in hospital and that I was mentally unwell. 'Oh Dad, just because you say *unwell*, doesn't make it sound any better.' I rebuked him.

'Billie, you *are* unwell, at the moment, ill sounds negative. Unwell sounds more positive, like- you will be well again. And you will be.'

'Okay, whatever you say. What did Mouseman say anyway?'

'*Mr.* Mouseman said he was very sorry to hear you are unwell, and he looks forward to seeing you back as soon as you are ready.'

I was taken aback. It was a nice of Mr. Mouseman to say that, it made me feel more positive that I might actually finish the course. I nodded and made an approving face. 'Okay, well that's nice,' I said.

'Yes it is. And he said that he thought the other students in your group might like to come and see you.'

I had to think about that. I wasn't sure I'd be well enough, and also it would mean that they would all know what was wrong with me. And what if Mum and Mr. Newell tried to gatecrash the visit, I would be mortified. 'I'll think about it,' I said.

'Alright, well let me know. Mr. Mouseman said he would say nothing to anybody unless you want him to.'

Dad also told Maddie at Bunnies that I was ill in hospital with a nervous breakdown. '*A nervous breakdown?* Dad, for goodness sake, it's not the nineteen-fifties. Goodness knows what Maddie must think. But he'd said it now, I could do nothing about it.

'She was very understanding on the phone,' Dad said, 'she wished you better quickly and she'll pay you sick pay, she said.'

'Oh, well okay, that's nice too.' I was relieved to be honest. Both college and work were taking it very well. I just hoped that I would be out and back on track as soon as possible.

Most of the others who were on the ward last time had gone on leave or been discharged. The only other person I recognised apart from Sandra, was Janet, but she kept herself to herself most of the time. I knew she could be volatile sometimes and the other patients avoided her, but this time she seemed quiet, just staying in her bedspace and only coming out for her meals. She had been in a long time this admission, Sandra told me. 'She has bi-polar, she told me once. She's been in and out of hospital since she was twenty. Her mood goes up and down dramatically, I don't know much about it to be honest, but I think she's down at the moment.'

'That's so sad,' I said. 'So much time out of her life stuck in here.' Janet must have been in her fifties by now. I couldn't imagine being in and out of hospital for all those years.

The time was passing so slowly, and with each day I became more worried about my future career. Ward round came and Dr. Khali suggested an injection every two weeks instead of tablets. I told her I didn't really want an injection and I would rather keep on the tablets. Dr Khali said there was a new tablet we could try with less side-effects and that I would have to be very careful to take it every day. She said, 'I feel that in the future, Billie, you will be fine, and we'll be able to reduce your medication. But for now, you must take it, or you will relapse again, and I don't want that for you.'

I knew I didn't want that either. So I agreed even though, I was still wary. But I did trust Dr. Khali with her soothing tone and her kindly expression. Dad assured her he would be more vigilant and make sure I was taking my medication.

That night, Mum was furious. *After all I've done for you Billie, carrying you for nine months, feeding you till I was red-raw, working every hour God sent to buy you all the things you desired, and now, now, you're agreeing to do what that quack Khali tells you. What's the matter with you? Are you stupid?* She went on and on and on like that all night. And every so often, Mr. Newell would stick his six penneth-worth in too. *'You listen to your mother Billie, she knows best.'* Even with my head under the pillow I could still hear them nagging and cajoling me and then laughing hysterically together. I kept telling them to shut up and leave me alone, but they wouldn't. I felt my head would burst.

And then, it must have been about three in the morning. I felt a tap on my shoulder. I emerged from under the pillow to see Janet staring down at me with wild, black eyes and her hair all over the place. I tried to keep calm and not appear afraid, even though I feared I might be about to die. But then, straightening her hospital nightie beneath her, she sat down heavily on my bed. 'You need to take the medication Billie,' she said, 'or you'll end up in and out of hospital for the rest of your goddamn life. Is this what you want? To be tormented by them voices every waking minute. You're ill Billie and no wonder, you had a full-on emotional trauma. I know about your mother, it's not surprising you've gone nuts, but you might be absolutely fine in the future. In the meantime, give yourself a break, take the friggin' medication and get on with your goddamn life.' She patted my backside through the duvet and smiled reassuringly, adding, 'I know what I'm talking about love.' Then she left me and went back to her own bed.

To say I was surprised by Janet's pep talk would be a bit of an understatement, I was shocked, but in a good way. I'd never heard Janet say that much before, and I had to admit what she said made sense. I did not want to relapse again and keep having to come back into hospital. Mum would have hated it if her disappearance caused me to keep getting ill. I had to get a grip on my life, easier said than done, after all, I had no real control over my voices- yet. But I knew I had to do all I could to try and get well again. I decided I would listen to Dr. Khali and Lorea. I wanted out of here as fast as possible. I wanted a career, a life, and most of all, I wanted to find out what happened to my mother.

Chapter 10

'Hey Mags, lend me one's red party frock will one?'

'Are you having a bloody larff Lizzie? That's my very best dress from Harvey bloody Nicks, you think I'm going to lend you that to spill your fucking caviar and chips down it? No bloody way, I'm afraid, darling.'

'Oh Maggie, don't be such a damn bore, I'll tell Daddy on you. Mean as shite you are, you old has-been,' she took a drag from her pencil and blew her smoke right in my face with a wide freckle-faced grin.

The Queen was sitting on my bed, I had not long returned from my indisposition and she, the little horror, had been having a fine old time with my wardrobe while I was incapacitated.

'I see one has already helped oneself to my platform Docs and my Chelsea Girl blouse, you really take the bloody biscuit you know.' I stubbed out my oil pastel on the bedside table laughing.

'Oh Lizzie, I'm sorry, one just couldn't help oneself, you have such a fine array of quality gowns to choose from. Pleeeaase let me borrow the red frock. I promise I won't spill caviar on it.'

I pulled myself up and out of the bed, went over to the wardrobe and picked out the red dress. 'Here darling, have the damn thing, it's too small for me now anyway. It's yours and don't forget who gave it to you.'

The Queen jumped up and grabbed the dress off me, 'oh Lizzie, you're an absolute bloody star. I will never forget you for this. Oh, what can one ever do to repay you?'

'Just enjoy the ball dear Lizzie, and make sure you don't miss the pumpkin ride back.'

The Queen hugged and kissed me and danced around the room holding the red dress against herself, imagining the ball or the local disco, whatever it was she was going to. And we fell on the bed laughing till we could hardly breathe.

'Is it a ball you're going to Lizzie?' I asked as we lay, side by side looking at the luminous stars on the ceiling.

'No, it's Gill's party.'

'Ahh, I see. A commoner's party, when is it?'

'On Saturday night at Saint Anne's church hall.'

'Ooh exciting, that'll be fun, have they got a sound system?'

'Yeah, her Uncle Clive is doing it, he's got his own portable disco.'

'Uncle Clive's disco eh? I wish I could come, sounds like you *will* be having a ball.'

Joni laughed turning her face toward me, 'I don't want you coming Mags, you'll cramp my style.'

'What? How dare you! It's ages since I've been to a party, please let me come.'

'No way, I'd be ashamed.'

'Ashamed now? Oh my God, after all I've done for you,' I smiled at her. 'Remember the parties we used to have at home?'

'Yeah,' Joni pulled herself up, she plumped up some cushions and we sat against them on the bed. 'Mum and Dad used to throw a lot of parties didn't they? I must have been very young, but I still remember them.'

'Yes they did,' I replied. 'Their parties were great, remember those maxi dresses Mum made for us to wear at one of our house parties? I felt fabulous, we looked amazing.' I smiled at the memory of dancing the night away on the bare wood floor.

'Uncle Des used to do the music at our parties. He was pretty good at it I have to admit. Haven't seen them for a long time, Des and Aunty Dawn and Rodney.'

'No thank God,' Joni laughed. 'They were a bit weird. Remember that time Rodney said Mum must be a ghost.'

112

'Urgh, he could be very unpleasant that's for sure.'

We went quiet then for minute or two, lost in our own thoughts and raking over old memories of happier times when Mum was here with us and we had nothing much to worry about.

'I miss her so much.' Joni started to cry.

'Oh Joni,' I put my arm around her. 'Me too.'

'I think about her all the time. And I dream about her all the time too.'

'I'm so sorry, Joni. All this time, I've been ill and in hospital and everything, I haven't been here for you.' I pulled her close feeling so bad about how overlooked Joni had been in all this. Yes, she had Dad and Aunty Jean to turn to. But she needed me, as sisters, we had so much in common, losing our mother being the biggest and most important thing. 'What do you dream?' I asked her.

'Mostly I dream that Mum is drowning. That she is in a lake or a pond or something, calling for me to help her, but I can't. I just watch her drown. It's horrible.'

I thought my heart would stop. I said nothing. I needed to think. *Was I going mad again? Did Joni really just say that?*

'Drowning?' I asked, looking for confirmation that I had heard her right.

'Yes, drowning, in all sorts of places, its different every time, a lake, the sea, a swimming pool. Usually the dream starts off happy and nice, but it always ends up horribly.'

113

I decided not to tell Joni about my own dreams which, it seemed, were identical to hers. I didn't want to freak her out because it was certainly freaking me out. Late into the night I wondered what on earth was going on. Eventually I decided I needed to try and find out how and why such a thing might happen. Did I know anyone who had knowledge of dreams, dreaming that kind of stuff? No, I didn't think so. Then I thought of the library. Perhaps I might find a book there with the information I wanted. I decided I would go and look tomorrow. I was still off college and work, recuperating for a week. Maddie was going to give me fewer hours at the café, just five hours on a Saturday. I was happy with that. Dr. Khali recommended reducing anything that might induce too much stress, so that I'd be less likely to become ill again.

The following day I took a bus to the library to look up dreams, hoping to find something that might explain the strange phenomena of having the same dreams as your sister. Apart from the two librarians, there were only a couple of people in the library that chilly Tuesday morning, an old man looking at the newspapers and a young mum with a little girl looking at an Andy Pandy book in the children's area. I searched the shelves that the librarian directed me to for books on dreams. There were a couple that looked promising, I picked them out and went over to an easy chair next to the old man. He glanced up from his newspaper as I sat down.

'Morning dear,' he said.

'Good morning,' I replied, beginning to flick through one of the dream books.

'Reading about dreams are you?' He said looking at my book choices.

'Oh- yes, I am, it's just an interest I have.'

'Strange things dreams, they tell you things you thought you didn't know. But actually you did know all along.'

I nodded, even though I had no idea what he was talking about. 'How do you mean?' I asked.

He put down his newspaper, clearly he had a lot to say on this subject, or he just fancied a full-on chat. 'Well, it's your own brain or mind, or whatever, isn't it? So you must have information stored there that you're unaware of, until it comes out in a dream. And you think, *how did I dream that when I don't know anything about it?* But the thing is, you *do* know about it you just don't realise it when you're *conscious*.'

'I see, yes,' I said. It did seem to make some sense. 'You seem to know a lot about dreams?'

He laughed, 'I'm an old man, I've dreamt a lot in my time.'

I smiled, turning back to my book. The old man stood and, picking up his coat and shopping bag, he said, 'goodbye dear. I hope you find the answers you're looking for.'

The books were interesting, but neither of them seemed to explain the kind of simultaneous dreaming that Joni and I were experiencing. I gave up eventually and went home thinking about what the old man had said. Could Joni and my dreams be linked to something we both knew, but subconsciously? I couldn't answer that. There were so many *don't knows* about it all. I got home and took Teddy for a walk around the park, still brooding about the *don't knows*. Nothing was clear, nothing made sense. Then I thought, right, stop thinking about this because it'll make you crazy. I decided I still wouldn't tell Joni, but that I would just do all I could to support her and help her feel better.

That Saturday, I returned to work at Bunnies with its steamy windows and its welcoming smell of toast and coffee. It was nice to see everyone again. I was ready to go back.

'Here she is! Billy Holiday,' exclaimed Lenny as I walked in the door. 'Ooh we've missed you Billie Holiday, the place has fallen apart without you. No one else can make coffee quite like you.'

I laughed as I tied my apron round my waist, 'ah thanks Lenny, that's nice of you to say.'

Maddie poked her head out of the kitchen. 'Hey Billie, great to see you back, how are you? Come on into the kitchen, we've something for you.'

'Hi Maddie,' I made my way to the kitchen. There was a tray of tall wine glasses, and Pete in full waiter's outfit with a tea-towel over his arm was pouring champagne into them.

'Welcome back,' said Maddie and handed me a glass of bubbly.

Pete took the tray around the café and gave one to Lenny and Fred, Tania, Graham, and a couple who were having lunch. I was quite touched, if a little embarrassed. 'Thank you everyone, that is very kind of you.'

'Nothing like a little champagne for lunch,' said Pete, taking off his black jacket, 'but now, I must get on with some frying.'

Soon Bunnies was back to its hustling, bustling self, full of customers, full of chatter and laughter and the clanking of pots and pans. I was tired at the end of the day, but it felt good, like I was doing something well. Perhaps I could even call it *happiness*, a feeling deep down, that at last, I might be living a *normal* life. Normal. A strange word, not very inspiring, but it's all I wanted. To live a normal life, mundane, maybe a little boring, but reasonably happy, with ups and downs that are manageable and resolvable. Normal, like everyone else. Well, everyone whose mother didn't disappear when they were twelve.

Aunty Jean was serving up dinner at our house when I got back from work. Dad and Joni were already eating.

'Hello love, how was it?' she said. 'I've made you egg, beans and sausage on toast for tea. Come and sit down.'

Dad grinned across the table at me and poured some tea.

Great, I thought, *just what I've been serving all day*. But I said, 'Thanks Jean, that looks amazing. Work was fine, I quite enjoyed it actually, everyone was really kind, they'd even got some champagne in.'

'Blimey,' Dad said, 'that's some café, can't think of many places would do that when you come back off sick.'

117

'I know, it was so nice, everyone was a bit tipsy by ten o'clock.' I squirted some brown sauce on my sausages and looked up at Joni. 'It's the party tonight isn't it Joni?'

'Yup, it sure is, I'm going to get ready now,' she shovelled the last forkful of beans into her mouth and got up to go upstairs.

'Want any help with your hair or anything?' I asked.

'No, I'm good thanks,' Joni called back as she ran up the stairs.

'*I'm good?*' Dad frowned, '*I'm good*. What's that supposed to mean?'

Aunty Jean laughed, pulling out a chair, 'its American isn't it Ron? The youngsters want to be American these days. It's because of *Fame*, they all love *Fame*.' And out of the blue she started singing the theme song to *Fame*. I thought she must have been at the sherry. Dad grunted and carried on eating.

Joni looked amazing in my ex red dress with its narrow straps over the shoulders and flouncy short Ra-Ra skirt, it suited her small frame and her skin tone. Aunty Jean suggested she put a cardi on, but Joni refused point blank. Her friend Sophie and her dad picked Joni up in a pink Ford Zephyr and Dad said he would collect them at eleven from Gill's house in the Ford Cortina. Like Cinderella, off she went to the ball, full of excitement and anticipation for the night ahead. I watched her go, laughing and joking with her friend. And I was so glad to see her living a good life, having fun as a teenager should, and glad that she was able to put behind her the anguish of all that had happened, at least for a little while.

118

The following Monday I returned to college. Like returning to Bunnies, it was good to see everyone again. The other students and Eric were kind and welcoming, and after all the initial greetings of *it's great to see you back* and *it's great to be back,* we all got on with making art. While I was away the class had been out and about drawing the old warehouses and dockland buildings, the remnants of our seafaring city. The theme was decay and dereliction.

'You can just do a portrait of me,' joked Greg.

Eric said that would be a step too far, that there was only so much dilapidation an artist could take. He suggested one or two of the others should come with me down to the docks so that I could make a few sketches, and they could do more if they liked.

Greg and Alice came with me, 'I need to do a few more sketches,' Alice said gathering up her pencils and oil pastels. 'Me too,' said Greg, and smiling, he leaned over to me and added, 'anything for a little trip out.' First we stopped off at a café for breakfast and had a little look around the boho shops for a new headscarf for Alice. We got to the docks around eleven am. The day was chilly and grey with looming clouds gathering above, a typical, gloomy March day. Alice wrapped her new, tie-die headscarf around her head tying it in a big droopy knot on top *a la* Bananarama. She looked *the biz* I thought, and I felt ashamed of my dreary grey sweatshirt, black jacket and black jeans, thinking I must overhaul my wardrobe and inject a little colour and style. I was supposed to

119

be a budding artist after all, I really should be dressing the part.

The local council had approved plans for some regeneration of the docklands and that was just beginning in a small part of the docks. But we headed for the more run-down, old, unused docks to make our sketches. Alice sat down on a wall and set out her pencils and oil pastels ready to start work. 'I love these old buildings, full of so much history, if only they could talk, what stories they could tell.'

'Ooh Alice, that's very thought-provoking for eleven in the morning,' Greg replied. 'No, I do know what you mean. So many years of trade, these docks must have been a hive of bustling activity over the centuries.' He opened his bag and pulled out his sketchbook and pencils, adding, 'I love drawing decay and dereliction, it's my forte.'

'Oh me too,' I smiled at him, he was funny in a very dry way and easy-going, he made us laugh that day as we sat on the chilly dock, drawing in our fingerless gloves.

As the day drew on, the light began to fade. The old dockland was an atmospheric place to sit and draw, full of shadows and ghosts and dark waters. As I put my charcoal to the paper, my eyes were drawn to the water in the dock, its blackness seemed impenetrable, it's depths unfathomable. I began to press my charcoal to the paper to replicate the darkness and the mystery of what may lie beneath. My hand worked faster and pressed harder, I needed to know what was beneath that water and the only way to do that was to depict it exactly as I saw it. And then, I don't know why, I drew a hand reaching out from the cold blackness of the water, a slim pale hand.

'That's interesting,' said Greg, 'I don't see it in the dock, but that hand is a very interesting addition, I like it.'

I was suddenly pulled back to reality. And I realised, with some embarrassment what I had done. 'Oh, my imagination is running away with me,' I said.

Alice leaned over to see, 'I like it too, it's very inventive, it'd be a good illustration for something, definitely. It reminds me of The Lady of the Lake.'

'Yes, it is a bit like that.' I laid down my charcoal and stopped scrubbing at the paper like a maniac. 'To be honest, I think it has come from a dream I had- or dreams, I should say.'

'Ooh, tell me more,' Alice replied, 'I love dreams, they're my thing, I've read a lot about them, it's so interesting interpreting them.'

'Really?' I turned to her, 'I dream a lot.' I was saying too much, and I knew it. I should keep this to myself, Alice would never be able to interpret my crazy dreams. But there was something about Alice that drew me to her, I trusted her, and Greg. But Alice, if I was going to talk to anyone about my dreams, it would be her.

Chapter 11

That Old Devil Called Love. The last of Billie Holiday's meandering notes drifted away across the café as Lenny, eyes closed, lost in the moment, nodded his head slowly in satisfaction. I smiled and placed his full English on the table in front of him. His eyes opened and, looking up, he said 'ah

Billie, our own Billie Holiday, what a wonderful morning this is.' He smiled, winked at me and lifted his cutlery to tuck in.

'Enjoy,' I said.

It was Saturday, late morning, a quiet day for some reason. 'Everyone must be having a lie-in,' Maddie commented.

'It's the football,' Pete reminded us, rolling his eyes in resignation that he would be missing the match.

'Urgh, football was never my thing,' Lenny chipped in, his mouth full of eggy toast.

'In this great footballing city?' Maddie said, placing his tea down on the table for him.

'Oh no, never could abide it. Cricket was more my thing. Lovely summer days, sitting out on the field in the fresh summer air, the players all in white, picnics, a cold beer. Much more civilised.'

'I can understand that,' said Tania from behind the counter. 'I don't like football either, prefer tennis.'

Graham was quiet, he carried on wiping tables, he didn't seem to be listening, lost in his own world.

'What about you Graham?' I asked, attempting to include him in the conversation. 'Do you like football?'

He looked up, drew in his breath. 'Er, not really bothered to be honest. I'm not really a sporty person at all.'

Pete popped his head out the kitchen, 'Ah aye, Graham, I thought you might be an ally for me, no one a football fan here? Outrageous.'

Graham smiled and picked up a sugar bowl, taking it to refill at the counter. 'Sorry Pete,' he looked apologetically towards the chef. 'My dad was a big footie fan,' he continued. 'But he was a pain in the arse. He had me and my brother in the local team, but he put so much pressure on us that we didn't enjoy it. I think he hoped we'd be good enough to make the bigtime,' he laughed, 'but he only ended up putting us right off.'

'Parents eh?' Maddie said. 'Trying to live out their dreams through their kids. My mum was a bit like that with netball, she thought I could go to the Olympics, can you imagine? Me!' She laughed raucously at the thought.

'Where's your mate Fred this morning?' I asked Lenny, realising that I hadn't seen him yet today.

'Not feeling too well this morning he said. I rang him earlier, but he was planning to stay in and rest, thinks he has a cold coming, or flu or something.'

'I hope he's alright,' I replied. 'The weather's turning isn't it? Flu season, perhaps its flu he's got.'

'Mmm maybe,' Lenny agreed.

Bunnies got busier that afternoon and then, despite my reduced hours, Maddie asked if I could stay till five. 'Say if you don't feel like it, honestly, it's just that I could do with going at four. I promised I'd pop in on Mum and have tea with her. So if you could stay, you could lock up with Graham and it'd save me that job. Would you mind? Honestly though, say

124

if you don't feel up to it. I really don't want you to feel you have to…'

I interrupted her in mid-flow, 'Maddie, its fine, it's no problem. I will close up with Graham. Go and enjoy time with your mum.'

She looked relieved, 'thank you so much, you're a lifesaver. My mum likes her tea early, usually her neighbour has tea on a Saturday with her but she's away this weekend. I'll do the takings, if you two could just clean and lock up, that'd be fantastic.'

So at four, Maddie left to go and have tea with her mum. A fleeting thought crossed my mind. How much would I love to go and have tea with *my* mum? It was a rhetorical question. The answer was un-put-into-wordsable. But I smiled at Maddie as she left and said, 'enjoy yourself,' and reassured her that we would be fine getting everything sorted. Lenny was given the biggest hints that it was time to go, but he didn't get them, or he pretended not to. So we gave him another coffee and cream on the house and cleaned up around him.

'It's not a bad place to work is it?' Graham said as he mopped the chocolate cake off the floor where some toddler had been sitting.

'No, not bad at all,' I agreed. 'In fact, I like it. It's my first job, could have been a lot worse.'

'Definitely.'

The cassette was still playing, Fleetwood Mac singing *Silver Springs,* as luck would have it. I locked the door and turned

125

the sign to *Closed*. Outside, the autumn evening was drawing in even though it was only four-fifteen. I loved the dark and the mist and the scent of burning leaves in the air.

'Ooh, we're having a lock-in,' laughed Lenny. 'Get the gin out then.'

I wished we did have gin, but I wasn't a big drinker. 'Shall we have a sneaky coffee?' I said to Graham.

He grinned, 'well I didn't get a break, did you? I think she owes us a coffee at least.'

So we sat down on the table near the back, with the lamp on and the door locked and Fleetwood Mac on the cassette and had two steaming mugs of coffee with cream, me and Graham.

'Do you think you'll stay here?' I asked him.

'What forever? No way, I'm hoping to go to college in September. But I'll work here temporary hopefully.'

'What do you want to study?'

'Journalism. I like writing, maybe music journalism, something like that.' He looked embarrassed, as if he shouldn't be thinking that, as if he shouldn't dare to have a dream like that.

'That's great, it sounds really interesting,' I said. 'I'm at the art college. I want to do illustration. You know, pictures for books, magazines, that kind of thing.'

Graham put down his mug. 'Wow,' he said, 'that's brilliant. You must be very good at art.'

'I don't know, I enjoy it, that's the most important thing.'

126

We supped our coffee quietly and across the room, Lenny appeared to be dozing in his chair. Graham and I smiled at each other, and I got up to unlock the front door.

'Lenny,' Graham was gently shaking the old man's shoulder. 'It's time to go home now, the café's closing.'

'Christmas, already?' Lenny came to, blinking, 'I must get to the shops.'

'No Lenny,' Graham reassured him, 'it's not Christmas, just time to go home, that's all.'

So the old man left, he only lived around the corner. Graham made sure he had his keys to hand and off he went. I finished cleaning up behind the counter, putting any left-over cupcakes in the fridge and wiping the filter coffee machine. And then, out of the blue, Graham said, 'are you feeling better now?'

I was a bit taken aback. And he added, 'I'm so sorry, that was a bit out of the blue. I just mean, are you ok now?'

'Yes, thanks Graham, I'm ok now.' I wondered how much he knew. Did he know I'd had a psychotic episode? That's what Dr. Khali called it. It sounded serious, it was serious, I knew that. But did he? I had no idea what he thought I'd been off sick with. So I just said, 'yeah, I'm fine thanks. Do you all know what was wrong?'

'Not really,' he answered. 'But you were off quite a while.' He paused. 'The thing is, Billie, I remembered your mum in the news. So I wasn't surprised when you were off for a while. It must be very hard dealing with something like that. It doesn't just go away.'

'No, it doesn't, you're right. It doesn't just go away.' I pulled a chair out; this was one of those conversations that needed a chair.

'I'm sorry Billie, I didn't mean to be nosey. It's just, my mum and dad, they split up when I was about eleven. And I saw her once since, then, never again. She didn't disappear. She just didn't want to see us anymore. So, yeah, that was hard. I think that's why I remembered your mum on the news, because it was around the same time that mine left.'

'Oh my God, I'm sorry Graham, that's awful.' I was shocked at what he had told me. What was wrong with me? I never really considered that other people had lost their mums too. Not in the same, mysterious, unresolved way that I had, but just as devastating, just as painful.

'Yeah,' Graham said, swilling the last cold dregs of coffee around his cup. 'What can you do? I'm eighteen now. It was a long time ago, She left, she didn't want us kids around, or Dad. You can't make someone love you or want you. But she had other problems of her own, I know that. She had alcohol problems. Maybe she thought she was doing the best thing for us.'

I nodded slowly, thinking about this. 'That sounds more understandable, Graham. That she didn't want it to affect you. Still very hard though for you, either way.'

Graham sighed, 'yeah, it is more understandable I guess.'

I put out my hand to take his cup and picked up mine to go to the kitchen, on the way I glanced at the clock. Five-thirty-five.

'Bloody hell, look at the time,' I exclaimed. 'Sorry Graham, it has been good talking, I must get home though. Dad'll be wondering where I am. And Aunty Jean will have tea ready.' I grabbed my coat, 'it'll be bloody, sausage and beans on toast again,' I said laughing.

Graham smiled, 'it has been nice talking, thanks Billie. Look, you go, I'll lock the door.' He stood up, scraping his chair on the stone floor.

'Ok, thanks Graham, see you next Saturday,' I said, as I scooted out the front door. Then, I stopped. I had a thought, and I popped my head back inside the café door. 'Hey Graham, fancy some sausage and beans on toast? There'll be enough, there's always too much.'

So Graham came back for tea, he telephoned his dad from our house to let him know. 'It's fine with Dad,' he said, 'he doesn't mind, he's watching the wrestling finals. I usually get a take-away on a Saturday, this is much nicer.' Aunty Jean smiled and set another place at the table. 'Well it's very nice to meet you Graham,' she said in an unusually refined tone of voice for her. Dad grinned at me and winked. I rolled my eyes thinking *oh for goodness sake Jean.* Joni was grinning too, and then she piped up, 'you're a bit younger than our Billie aren't you?'

'I think I am, slightly. I'm eighteen,' Graham answered politely.

'Oh, our Billie's nineteen, so you're a bit young for her.' Joni was staring at Graham in an unnerving manner. But Graham smiled at her disarmingly and nodded. 'Yes, I can see you must think that, but I've just come for tea. Billie very kindly invited me. I hope that's alright.' He looked up as Aunty Jean put a plate of food in front of him. 'Of course it's alright,' she said, 'you are very welcome Graham. Take no notice of Joni, she's a cheeky madam, she needs to mind her tongue.' She looked over to Joni with a stern expression, 'you eat your dinner,' she told her sharply.

Graham stayed to watch *Saturday Night at the London Palladium* and after that he left to go home. 'Ah, thanks very much Billie,' he said on the doorstep. 'I've really enjoyed this evening.'

'So have I,' I replied. 'It was nice.'

'Yeah, it really was.' He shuffled a little in the chill night air and shoved his hands deep into the pockets of his donkey jacket. 'Bye then, Billie, see you at Bunnies next Saturday, have a good week.'

I nodded and smiled. 'You too, see you then Graham, goodnight.' I watched as he disappeared out the gate and into the darkness.

The following Saturday at Bunnies, Lenny told us that Fred had been taken into hospital with pneumonia. He was very worried about him and wanted to go to the hospital to see him. I told Lenny that if he wanted to go and see Fred I was sure my Dad wouldn't mind giving him a lift, and I would come with him.

'Really? Would he really not mind? That would be lovely. I can't manage the buses these days, but I would like to see Fred. I really would. To be honest, I'm quite worried. I've seen what pneumonia can do, especially to someone Fred's age.'

Maddie packed up some pasties and cupcakes for us to take to Fred, and that evening I asked Dad if he could take Lenny and me to see him at the hospital the next day, which was Sunday. Dad, being Dad, said 'yes' without hesitation. So I rang Lenny on the number he had given me and arranged to pick him up the next day at eleven in the morning.

Fred looked at death's door and, if I'm honest, I was quite shocked. He was pale with a yellowish tinge, and his cheeks had sunk in to reveal the skeletal look of a person found in a peat bog after three thousand years. This was not a nice comparison to make I know, but I couldn't help it. As we approached, Fred's eyes opened, they seemed very light blue, lighter than I remembered them. He smiled very weakly. 'Lenny, hello. And, erm Bonny, hello. How nice to see you both.'

'Billie,' said Lenny, 'her name's Billie, not Bonny.'

I touched, Lenny's arm, 'it's okay, don't worry,' I said.

But he continued, 'it's Billie after Billie Holiday, you remember now eh? Fred?'

Fred drew in his breath, 'oh Billie, I'm sorry, I thought it was *Bonnie* after Bonnie Tyler,' his voice was little more than a

131

whisper. I felt bad that he was wasting his last dregs of energy on my name and namesakes.

'Honestly, Fred,' I leaned nearer to him, 'don't worry. *Billie-Bonnie*, who cares?'

He tried to laugh but it resulted in a coughing fit, and I seriously thought that was it, I had killed him. A young nurse rushed over and popped an inhaler into his mouth and thankfully he seemed okay after a couple of puffs. I sighed with relief. 'I'm just going to nip to the loo,' I said. 'You two have some time, I won't be long.' With that, I nipped to the café across the road for a coffee and a cigarette. Boy, I hated hospitals with their stinking disinfectant and their blue painted walls. I decided I'd wait a little while and then go back to meet Lenny. I found a table in the window. The view outside was no oil painting that's for sure, rain drizzled down the glass, and beyond was a dreary sea of grey, cars splashing along a wet, tarmac road, past a mud-grey hospital building. Dad had buzzed off to town to meet Aunty Jean for lunch, he said he'd pick us up in a couple of hours. So I sat with my coffee *au lait* and a newspaper from the wall rack and enjoyed being inside a warm café not having to serve anyone.

When I returned to the ward, it was all happening. Curtains drawn around beds, nurses running around with pieces of equipment, urgent voices saying things like- *stand clear* and *all visitors please wait in the corridor.* I saw Lenny sitting in the corridor. 'Gosh, what's going on?' I asked as I sat down next to him. He seemed shocked, his voice was shaky, 'it's

Fred, he took a turn for the worse. I don't think he's going to make it.'

I put my hand on his. 'Oh God, no, I'm so sorry Lenny, that's awful. And I'm sorry I went out. I should have stayed with you both.'

'Oh, Billie, don't you worry, when you've got to go, you've got to go. There's nothing you can do about it.'

I looked down at the blue linoleum feeling guilty about the coffee *au lait*.

When Dad came to pick us up, Fred had died. Lenny and I were both upset of course, but I was glad that Lenny had been with him. 'He had no other family that I know of,' he told us. 'His wife died a few years ago. So I am very grateful that we were here, and I was able to see him before he went. And that's thanks to you, Billie and your Dad.'

It was a subdued car ride home. We invited Lenny back to our house for a cup of tea, but he preferred to go home. So Dad and I went into his house with him and made him a cup of tea there. And we sat together for a while in his tiny lounge which smelt a tad of mildew and ginger nuts.

'I'll miss old Fred, he was a good chum,' Lenny told us. 'We fought in the war together you know. Landed on the beach together on D-Day. It was like hell on earth, the things I saw, I never could talk about. Not ever. I thought my life was over. And it nearly was, but he saved me, Fred, yes, he saved my life. Pushed me out of the line of fire, he did.' The old man nodded his head slowly. Lost in memories, he was faraway

133

amidst the horror of battle, his brown eyes brimming with the tears of remembrance.

And suddenly I saw the young man he once was. Petrified beyond all imagining, but trying to be brave, wondering how on earth he was there when he should have been home with his family, training to be a baker or a plumber or something, anywhere but on a godforsaken beach, with his mates being shot to pieces. I was hardly able to speak for the lump in my throat. I had no idea Lenny and Fred had lived through so much history together.

'You were brave men,' Dad said.

'*Fred* was brave,' Lenny said. 'I was frightened as a kitten, but Fred said to me, *chin up Len, we've got a job to do*. Then he saved my life and we've been pals ever since. Till now.' And he pulled out a hankie from his pocket and he wept and wept.

Chapter 12

'I have heard of such things,' Alice said slowly, thoughtfully, as she sipped her grape juice. It was breaktime and we were sitting in a quiet corner of Buckland's Bar. Teddy was at my feet, begging for bits of toast.

Alice continued, 'I think when two people have similar dreams it's because they have a similar memory that's triggering them.'

'That makes sense,' I agreed. 'But the thing is, I just can't pinpoint a memory that might have triggered such a specific type of dream.' I hadn't told her the details of the dreams yet, and how alike both Joni and my dreams really were. 'It's to do with my mum, you see.' I continued. 'I don't know if you know about her disappearing when we were younger.'

'Ah yes,' Alice nodded and looked at me with a warmth in her brown eyes. 'I do know, yeah. I didn't like to bring it up unless you did. But yes, I had heard. I'm so sorry, I can't imagine how hard that must have been.'

I nodded. 'Thanks Alice. You see, my dreams are always about my mum struggling in water. She could be in a pool or a lake, the sea, any expanse of water. The dreams usually start off nice, happy, bright, like there'll be lots of flowers and maybe singing and music. But every time, the scene soon turns dark and ominous, and it always ends up with Mum drowning.' I paused and took a sip of my hot coffee. 'The really strange thing is, that not long ago, I found out my sister has been having exactly the same kind of dreams. I should call them nightmares really because that's what they are.'

'Oh my God, that is very strange,' Alice's eyes widened, she put down her cup. 'Where were you staying when your mum disappeared? Was it near the sea, or a lake or river, anything like that?'

'Well it was a couple of miles from the sea, but no, it was a farm inland, there were no lakes or rivers near us I don't think.' I dropped a piece of toast into Teddy's mouth.

'It sounds like there must have been something that's triggered you and your sister to dream the same type of dream. Something, obviously to do with water. I'm sorry, I'm not much help am I?' Alice frowned apologetically.

'Honestly Alice, you are being *very* helpful,' I reassured her, 'it's actually, really nice to about this with someone. I haven't told anyone before. Even my sister, Joni, doesn't know we have the same dreams. I haven't told her because I felt it might just worry or upset her.'

Alice raised her eyebrows. 'Really? I think maybe you *should* tell her. Perhaps it would reassure her, like you found it good to talk about it. She might need to talk about it with you. It might help her to think she's not dreaming these scary things on her own.' It was a good point Alice was making. We drained our cups and returned to college. I thought about what she had said and realised that Alice was probably right. Perhaps it would help Joni to talk about our dreams, perhaps it

136

would help us both. I decided I would talk to her about it that evening.

When I got home I was greeted by Joni with the news that Dad was going out on a date.

'What? Are you serious? Who with? You *are* joking?'

'No I'm not,' she pulled me into the kitchen where Dad was in front the of the cooker looking at his reflection as he straightened his tie.

'Dad, where are you going?' I asked, dropping my bag onto the table with an accusatory thump.

'Hello Billie, what's she been telling you?' Dad didn't look round.

'She told me you're going on a *date*.'

Dad turned to look at Joni, wagging his finger at her. 'You're a little troublemaker Joni.' Then he looked to me, 'it's not a date love. I'm just meeting Pat for a whist drive.'

'A *whist drive*?' I screwed up my face. 'You never do things like that.'

'No but she invited me, and I thought, well perhaps I should get out a bit, be sociable. It's not just Pat, there's a few from work going. It's not a *date*, Bill. I don't want dates. Good God, I'm a married man.' He smiled at me and patted my shoulder as he reached for his jacket off the back of the door. 'I won't be late back. There's spag bol in the fridge for you.'

I raised one eyebrow as he left the house without a backward glance. I had thought before about the possibility of Dad finding someone new. Going on a date, wanting a relationship

137

with another woman. I hoped he wouldn't, but really I couldn't expect that he would wait forever when it was clear Mum wasn't coming back. She had been gone nearly six years now. I had some recollection that after seven years, the law assumes a missing person is dead, and you are free to remarry, I'd heard it on *Poldark*. So legally, in another year or so, Dad could remarry if he wanted, it was a sobering thought. I had mixed feelings about it. But still, tonight was just a whist drive, he had said he didn't want dates. So I decided to think no more about it and eat my spag bol with Joni.

'Hey, Joni, are you still having weird dreams?' I asked her as we ate.

'God yes, all sorts of things. I dreamt Mum was on a moor with Kate Bush the other night. Kate was doing that weird dancing she does and singing, I love that song, about Cathy. But then Mum started sinking in a bog. Kate couldn't hear her calling for help cos it was too wild and windy, and she was singing too loud. I was trying to tell her, *Mum's drowning in a bog*, but she couldn't hear me either. Then Mum's head disappeared under the sludge, it was awful. I felt sick. Then I woke up.'

I had stopped eating and was staring open-mouthed at Joni. 'That is one hell of a dream, good grief. I wish Kate Bush featured in my dreams.'

'More of a nightmare though really,' Joni twirled her spaghetti round her fork.

'Yes, it's awful, horrible, I know.' I breathed in deeply, preparing to disclose the truth of our simultaneous dreaming. 'Actually Joni. It's very strange you know, because I have dreams about Mum drowning too. Just like you.'

Joni looked up, puzzled. 'Do you? It must be because I told you about my dreams.'

I shook my head. 'No, I was already having my dreams before you told me. I didn't say anything because it was so odd. I didn't want to frighten you.'

She laughed, 'I'm not frightened. But it's too weird. Why do you think we both have dreams about Mum drowning?'

I told Joni about what Alice had said, and she agreed that it was a good hypothesis. 'But I don't know, why *drowning*? *Drowning*. Do you think she drowned somewhere?'

'I don't know Joni,' I started clearing the plates off the table. 'But if she did drown,' I continued, 'how do we know to dream about it? It makes no sense. I don't believe in supernatural hocus pocus. There must be a reason behind it. Like Alice said, we must have some common memory, something that our brains are both trying to tell us.'

Dad got back from the whist drive about half past twelve, much the worse for wear. I was in bed, but I heard him fall up the stairs and stagger across the landing to his room. He was still in bed when I was leaving for college the next morning. I popped my head round his door. 'A good night was it Dad? You're going to be very late for work you know,' I said. He

139

raised his head off the pillow squinting at me with red eyes and groaned. I smiled and left to go for the bus.

At college that day we carried on working on our theme of dereliction and decay. Greg, at his drawing board next to me, was painting with acrylics on a huge piece, all in greys, deep blues and blacks. 'It's a depressing sight, but I'm quite enjoying doing it,' he told me.

I was using mixed media to layer up my *hand rising out of the dock* piece, it was a work in progress. I wasn't sure about it at all. But I had no other ideas, so I was ploughing on with it. I felt I was reaching a bit of an impasse. And I said this to Eric as he wandered around checking on everyone's work.

'Well, I can see the texture of your piece is very interesting. The water definitely has depth and a certain foreboding quality which I like very much.' He leant forward to inspect the thin, white hand rising from the swirling black water. 'Hm, interesting,' he commented, 'what's this about? Very Lady of the Lake-esque. Is that the effect you were after?'

'I don't really know,' I answered, unhelpfully. 'I don't know what effect I was going for. It just sort of- happened.'

Eric continued to look and as he did, I knew that it was, of course, Mum's hand reaching out for help. 'It's my mum,' I said. The room was quiet anyway with everyone working busily, but after I said that, it seemed to suddenly go completely silent. 'Oh okay. I see,' Eric shifted uncomfortably.

But he did not see. No one saw, even when they said *I see*.

140

'I don't think anyone really sees,' I said rubbing the white and black oil pastel together on the paper to create a stormy grey sky. 'No one *really* sees,' I repeated. 'I've put her there, so everyone can see her like I do. Drowning.' I looked up. Greg, next to me was nodding his head as if he understood or was at least trying to understand. I could just see Marnie's black hair and her green eyes blinking opposite me, peering over the top of her drawing board.

'I'm sorry love,' Eric said, 'I won't ask anymore, unless you want to talk about it.'

I was overcome with embarrassment, *why on earth did I say that?* 'No, I'm sorry, I shouldn't have said all that,' to my horror I thought I was about to start crying, I fought to contain myself.

Alice was suddenly there, by my side, 'of course you should Billie, if that's what you needed to say. Art is nothing if it's not honest. You were being honest Billie. You are putting yourself into your work, there is nothing more truthful than that.' She put an arm around my shoulder, it made me feel safe and supported. She took me and Teddy off to the stock cupboard where we were surrounded by boxes of paint and paper, it was a warm, comforting place with two chairs for occasions such as this.

'Are you okay?' Alice asked.

'Yeah, I'm fine, I just had a bit of a wobble, I don't know why.' I replied.

'It's understandable after all you've been through,' she said.

141

'Perhaps I shouldn't have put that hand in the picture. It's not how I want to remember my mum. It's just what I see in my dreams. I don't even know how she died; we don't know that she drowned.'

'Well, maybe you are just exploring that in your picture. Bringing your dreams out into the open probably takes some of the fear out of them.' She tilted her head, questioningly, 'maybe?'

'You're very perceptive Alice. I think you are definitely right. It's certainly brought my dream out into the open today. Poor Eric, I think I embarrassed him. I feel awful.'

'Don't feel awful, he's alright. He'll be down The Craic later forgetting all about it.'

I smiled, she was certainly right about that, so we returned to the art room. Everyone was busy getting on with their work and Teardrop Explodes was playing on the cassette machine. Eric was at his desk, he looked up, 'okay love?'

I went over to him. 'Yes thanks Eric, sorry about that.'

'God Billie don't apologise. You can say anything you like to me, put me in my place, I don't mind, as long as you're okay. I'm not the most articulate person in the world, but thank God, we have Alice.'

I went back to work, adding more depth and highlighting the sky and the tips of the water with white pastel. The surrounding warehouses loomed over the dock like monsters with a thousand window eyes. The scene became more and more ominous and more and more like the dreams that had

142

haunted me every night. There was something cathartic about working on the picture with its layers of thick oil pastel, soft pencil and charcoal. I used my fingers to smooth and smudge the textures together. And I thought, *if only* I could lift Mum's delicate white, hand out of the water and bring her back, warm her, hold her, comfort her, ask her where she had been all this time. *If only* I could take her home where she should be.

So the whole group knew now that I was the girl whose mum went missing when she was twelve. And that I had not survived the trauma, that I had been in a psychiatric hospital and still remained very vulnerable to illness. I had exhibited my innermost terror by drawing my mother drowning for all the group to see. I realised, that in a way, I had trusted this group now with my deepest sense of loss and fear.

Life had its ups and downs, but mainly it was good. I loved art college and I enjoyed working at Bunnies. I had friends and family who cared about me. I kept on, hanging on, trying to live well and stay well. But always in the background was Mum. The mystery of her disappearance never went away, or the shock of her loss. Or the *if onlys*. After six years, *if only* was part of me now, intrinsic in every cell and in my blood.

March came to an end and at last, the weather began to warm up. One early evening in April our group were all at The Craic when Greg said, 'I've got an old van and I'm not afraid to use it.' We waited, for a bemused minute or two until he explained that he would drive us all for an unofficial field trip to the Lake District if we fancied it. We all fancied it.

'That's the best idea you've had so far this year,' Valerie told him.

'Great stuff, where will we stay?' asked Mike. 'I can bring a tent.'

But there was no need for tents thank goodness. Greg was a keen rock climber apparently and knew of a rock-climber's cottage at the base of *The Old Man of Coniston* where we could stay. 'It's very basic,' he warned us. 'Nothing fancy, at all, but we'll be outside most of the time anyway.'

Our whole group of eight were keen to go, Greg of course, Mike, Valerie and Alice, Rob, June, Marnie and me. We agreed the best day to go would be during the Easter holiday in the middle of April which was only ten days away. My excitement grew, anticipating my first ever holiday with friends.

Since Mum disappeared we had not had a proper holiday. Dad had taken Joni and me away for a weekend now and then to Wales or Shropshire, but none of us could face more than a few days away. It didn't seem right somehow, I was always afraid that Mum might come home while we were away and think we had forgotten her, that we'd gone off having a good time without her. Though I knew, in my heart, that was never going to happen.

Chapter 13

I told Maddie I wouldn't be able to work the Saturday after next. She was fine about it and said I deserved a holiday.

'It's supposed to be a field trip, but I doubt we'll do much work,' I told everyone.

'You'll all have a great time,' Pete commented. 'I'm quite jealous to be honest. Long time since I went away with mates, it's only ever the wife and kids now.' He looked wistful at the memory of his long-past holidays with the lads.

'Oh for goodness sake,' Maddie rebuked him. 'You should be happy to be away with your lovely family Pete. Some of us don't even get a holiday at all.'

Pete rolled his eyes and disappeared back into the kitchen.

The bell on the café door rang out as Lenny came in. I had visited him at home a few times in the three weeks since Fred died, but this was the first time he had been back to the café. Maddie immediately went over to offer her condolences and find him a table. I poured him a coffee and took it over with some cream.

Lenny smiled up at me. 'Hello Billie Holiday. Thank you love.' He looked brighter than I'd expected.

'How're you doing Lenny?' I asked.

'Not bad, really. I'm alright. I was very upset about Fred as you know. But I've been getting on with things. I've joined a dating agency actually.'

'*A what?*' I resisted the urge to laugh, but I couldn't hide my astonishment.

'Yes, a dating agency, it's alright Billie love, you can laugh if you want,' and he smiled at me as he pulled out a leaflet from his coat pocket. ***Love Interests*** it said at the top in red bubble writing. 'I'm meeting someone here for lunch in actual fact.'

I couldn't quite believe what I was hearing. Lenny was certainly not letting the grass grow since Fred died. I was surprised, and then pleased. 'Well, good on you,' I said, and I stood there grinning like a Cheshire Cat, till Maddie called me to get the bread out of the freezer.

We had a few customers coming in and out, and every time the bell rang I looked to see if it was Lenny's date arriving. Then, the bell on the door dinged around one thirty. I was just picking up some plates of food off the counter and paused for a moment to check out who was coming in. It was a tall man, he was wearing a long green coat and a hat, a kind of trilby I think you call it. I carried on arranging the plates on my arm and swerved around the counter to deliver them to their table, then I realised the tall man had gone over and was talking to

146

Lenny. I took the plates to their appropriate table and kept glancing over to see what was going on at Lenny's table.

The tall man must be a friend of Lenny's, I thought. He had sat himself on the chair opposite Lenny. *Oh no*, I thought, *Lenny will have to tell him to move, he's waiting for his date.* And then suddenly the lightbulb came on in my dimwit brain and I realised, the tall man *was* the date.

'Billie, this is Sam,' Lenny introduced me as I went to take their order. He looked to his lunch date and said, 'Sam, this is Billie, Billie Holiday I call her. She was named after the great songstress. And she's the best waitress in town.'

I grinned, 'oh Lenny, give over. Nice to meet you Sam. What can I get for you both?'

They made their order and I returned to the kitchen.

'Who's that with Lenny?' asked Maddie.

'Oh, a new friend I think, Sam, he seems very nice.'

'Aah good, I'm glad Len's getting out and about again. He's looking well,' and she leaned backward to peer out the kitchen door at the two men who were chatting and laughing like they'd been friends for years.

Later that afternoon during a quiet moment, Maddie told me to get a coffee and a sandwich and take a break. I sat on the high bar table in the corner which was supposed to be reserved for staff breaks but was usually utilised for excess customers. Graham was just finishing up after his break. 'Oh here Billie, sit here,' he pulled out the other stool next to him. 'I've got something to ask you actually,' he went on, 'Echo and the

147

Bunnymen are playing at the Hacienda in July. Do you fancy coming with me? I mean, say no if you don't, it was just an idea.' He looked down, a little embarrassed, and wiped the last bit of bean juice off his plate with some toast. I liked Echo and the Bunnymen, well, what I'd heard of them anyway, which wasn't much. But I did fancy going to a concert. It was time I got out and about and enjoyed the burgeoning talent of new and upcoming artists. Then I thought again, *did I want to go with wet-behind-the-ears Graham?* I inwardly reprimanded myself. I had not thought of him as wet-behind-the-ears at all since our conversation that evening in March, when he had come home for tea at our house. I had only thought of him as Graham. Nice, friendly, not-bad-looking Graham who had lost his mother too. So I said, 'yes I'd love to come with you Graham. Thanks for asking me.' He nodded, grinned and jumped down from his stool, then picking up his plate and cup he said, 'great, I'll order the tickets next week.'

I couldn't wait till July for the concert, but on the other hand, I could wait. I wanted time to slow down because, come July, my foundation course would be finished, and a long summer would lie ahead, a prelude to who-knows-what in September. I didn't know where I would be then, and the thought scared me. Eric encouraged us to look at degree courses around the country, but I knew I didn't want to leave the safety of my hometown, pathetic as it may seem. I had an ingrained fear that Mum might come back, and wonder how I could have gone off when she was missing. I was eligible for a small grant and if I lived at home I'd have no accommodation fees. So I applied for the degree course at the college and waited for an interview date.

A few others from our group had also applied to stay at the same college, June, Valerie, Greg and Alice. I was pleased about that because they were quickly becoming my closest friends, besides Graham. Oh, and Cheryl from schooldays, but I didn't see much of her since she hooked up with a bad boy from Manchester. Last I heard she had moved in with him and was having a baby much to Aunty Jean's horror.

The day approached when we would be going up to *The Old Man of Coniston* on our unofficial field trip. I was excited, the whole group was excited. Even Joni was excited for us. 'You'll have to take your swimming costume,' she told me. 'There's lots of lakes up there to swim in. And you'll need hiking boots, a fleece, a flask, a compass and a waterproof jacket.'

'Gosh, Joni, since when have you been so well informed on what's needed for a country break?' I remembered the totally inappropriate clothing and footwear of our childhood holidays. 'I have a list of what I need for our school trip to Yorkshire,' she explained. 'We need all those things. Well, not the swimming costume but the other things.'

Dad took a deep draw on his cigarette and turned the page of his newspaper at the kitchen table. 'Blimey, I better start saving up,' he muttered under his breath.

I couldn't afford all those things on Joni's list, but I did invest in a jacket and some walking boots with some help from Dad. They weren't the most attractive things in the world, but I guessed it wasn't going to be a fashion show. When the day came, it was bright and sunny. Spring was in the air, and I had a spring in my step as I skipped out of our gate like a newborn lamb with my rucksack on my back to jump in the van with the others who were waiting. Aunty Jean, Dad and Joni waved us off and we were away, windows down, flying up the motorway blasting out Bow Wow Wow on the cassette player singing *Go Wild in the Country* and letting that holiday vibe take hold, good and proper.

Basic was the word. It was the word Greg had used to describe the climber's cottage and it was definitely the most accurate word. In fact, *grotty* might have been even more accurate.

'Oh my God,' was all June could say, as she inspected the cooker which was coated in what looked like grime dating back to the eighteenth century.

'I like it,' Valerie said, 'we'll be out most of the time anyway, it's fine for our needs.'

'There's no shower, by the way,' interrupted Greg.

'Oh,' Valerie re-evaluated her previous comment, 'is there a B&B nearby?'

I was keeping quiet. I was tired, but also, I didn't care how grotty it was in the cottage, I was just glad to be here with friends. I knew we were going to enjoy this trip despite the

150

basic accommodation. We sorted out where we would all sleep. There were two big rooms upstairs, like dorms, one for the boys and one for the girls. The beds were just big wooden slatted things on the floor we had to cover them with groundsheets and our sleeping bags. They'd be fine. And once we had put all our stuff away we sorted out some dinner. It was a huge pan of tuna mush which Valerie and June had thrown together. I cut up some bread and opened the wine and beer. And once the food was ready we all sat outside in the evening sun and ate and drank and laughed and listened to the silence and the water splashing over the rocks in the little stream near the cottage. I thought I was in heaven.

We stayed out as darkness fell, getting tipsy on cheap alcohol and smoking roll-ups. I pulled on my fleece when it started getting chilly and, as the others chatted on, I gazed up at the clear, starry night sky swirling above us like the Van Gogh painting. Later, we cleared up the dinner things and one by one we all drifted off to bed, it wasn't late, but we agreed it would be good to get up early and make the most of our days.
'What's that noise?' Valerie whispered from the end bed.
'Erm, what noise?'
'Scratching, listen.'
'Oh my God.'
'Rats.'
'Fuck.'
We listened, the scratching went on, with the occasional squeak.

'I can't sleep with rats.' Marnie complained, her voice muffled inside her sleeping bag.

'They're under the floorboards, they can't get us,' June tried to reassure us.

'Rats are very clean and intelligent,' said *Mother Earth* Alice, appealing to our animal-loving sides.

So all in all, none of us had a good night's sleep and we woke around eleven. Downstairs, Mike, Greg and Rob were munching on bacon butties.

'Hey, hope you saved us some,' I said, as myself and the other four girls appeared, unwashed and unbrushed, feeling like shit, but really not caring anymore. We had braved the rat room and survived. Now we were ready to get out there and embrace nature in all its glory.

So after our breakfast we looked at a huge map that Greg spread out on the grass outside. And eventually, we all decided to go walking to a tarn called Goat's Water. The lads packed their climbing gear and us girls packed our cozzies, we were nothing if not ambitious. We planned to do some abseiling, but really all I wanted to do was lie in the sun and have a dip in the mountain tarn. We drove in the van to the nearest car park; from there it was a steep climb up to the lake. It felt good though, walking in the sharp, mountain air, our boots crunching along the stony path, miles and miles of open space around us and white-tipped peaks fading into the distance.

We stayed for hours there at Goat's Water, I could hardly comprehend the beauty of the place. Greg and Rob were experienced climbers and went off to climb the steep mountainside which rose up from the far side of the tarn. The rest of us lay around in the wiry grass surrounding the water's edge, venturing out occasionally for a swim. The waters of the tarn were like ice, and the further in we swam, the deeper and darker they became. Scary at first, but it was okay. I was safe with the others, I knew that. I floated on my back, the black water behind me, blue sky and mountains above me. And I thought about my mum and wondered if she knew I was here, in this exquisite place, thinking about her.

The days dawned warm and bright. They were days spent climbing waterfalls and bathing in blue, marbled pools, days of sunbathing, stretched out on huge prehistoric boulders which had lain for millennia on plateaus high amongst the mountains. And evenings spent sitting out under the stars or in village pubs, drinking, talking, laughing. There was a lot of laughing. I had made friends for life. The kind of friends you might not see for years as lives take different paths, but when you meet again it's like yesterday, as though no time has passed at all. You are still friends, always.

Spring moved into summer and our college course ended. Some of us lived in the same city and some further away, but we all agreed to stay in touch and meet up over the summer. The foundation course had been a great year and we celebrated and said our goodbyes with a good night out at The

Craic with Eric and some of the other tutors. And that was it. College was over for now. I felt a little empty and sad, even though I knew I'd be coming back in the autumn. Everything would be quieter now for me, less routine, less things to occupy my mind. I was a little scared, but at the same time, I was looking forward to the summer stretching ahead of me, with all its possibilities.

The hazy, lazy days of summer rolled by, sapping the energy of the old and filling the young with the heady joy of being off school with all the time in the world for swimming, picnics and holiday TV. Mostly, my summer was spent either sweltering in Bunnies or walking Teddy in the local park.

'Only a week to go before our concert,' Graham reminded me one evening as we were finishing up at the cafe.

I raised my eyebrows and stopped to think for a second. *Concert?* Oh yes, Echo and the Bunnymen. 'Yes, I can't wait,' I replied, as if I hadn't forgotten.

'You'd forgotten,' said Graham.

'No I had not.'

'Yes you had.' He smiled as he pulled on his jacket and we left the café, turning the key in the front door. 'Don't worry, it's a long time since I booked them. Are you still sure you want to come?'

'Yes, of course I'm sure. I'm looking forward to it.'

'Okay, that's good, so am I.'

I hadn't really forgotten about the concert, I just had so many other things crowding into my mind over the past month that it had been pushed to the back burner. Now that Graham had reminded me, thoughts of the concert were now reignited on the front burner and my excitement began to build again like a slow heat under the pressure cooker. I switched the radio on when I got home hoping that I'd catch a song by Echo and the Bunnymen, but unfortunately all they were playing was The Beatles and Cilla as usual. I rolled my eyes and turned the radio off.

'Oi! Put it back on,' Joni ordered 'I was listening to that.'

'No you weren't,' I retorted, 'I only just put it on.'

'Yes and I was listening to Michelle Ma Belle, it's my favourite song of all time. Put it back on.'

'Favourite song of all time,' I mocked, 'what about *Green Door?*'

'Put the radio back on love,' Dad chipped in. So I put it back on just in time for the last God-awful fake-French note.

Fortunately the following Saturday, Graham brought a cassette of Echo and the Bunnymen into Bunnies to get us in the mood for the concert which was on the following Tuesday.

'What's this racket love?' Lenny asked as I put his coffee down in front of him.

'It's a Liverpool band, Lenny, what do you think?'

'Bloody awful. What's 'e saying? *Spare us the Cutter*? What in heaven's name is that supposed to mean?'

Sam piped up, 'it's about Maddie in the kitchen, wielding the bread knife.' They both roared with laughter at this, I smiled and nodded.

'Seriously though love, it's not very cheerful is it?' Lenny continued, as he stuffed a piece of toast in his mouth.

'I haven't got a clue what it's about,' Sam said, 'but I'm sure it's not meant to be cheerful.'

Lenny took a slurp of his coffee. 'Oh, is that right. Well, each to their own I suppose. I'll stick to our Billie Holiday I think,' he said, winking at me.

Graham shot me a grin from behind the counter and I wandered around wiping a few tables. It was a quiet day; I supposed a lot of people were away on holiday. And I thought about my little holiday to the lakes with my college friends. And for a minute, I was drifting on Goat's Water again, my back against the deep black waters and nothing but blue sky and mountains above me.

It was over a year now since my *nervous breakdown* as Dad called it. And that week I had an appointment with Lorea. Over the past six months, Dr. Khali had slowly reduced my medication to the bare minimum, and I seemed to be doing okay on it. I hadn't had any more voices or odd thoughts about agony aunts, or anything like that, so Dr. Khali was thinking of stopping the tablets altogether. She thought that I had had a 'one-off' psychotic episode brought on by trauma and that I might never have one again. 'It's quite rare, but it certainly does happen,' she told me. But first she wanted me to see Lorea again. No doubt so that she could delve amongst my innermost neurons and discover any strange antics going on there that may surface when the tablets stopped.

156

'I feel fine,' I told Lorea in the comfort of her tiny grey and yellow office up on the fourth floor of the hospital. The sun shone in through the window and bathed the city in a little winter warmth. 'I haven't had any problems at all for a long time. Not one. No voices, no agony aunts, no nothing. Just the usual niggles of life that everyone has to deal with.' I put my coffee cup down on a *Love Is...* coaster.

'Sounds like you're doing well,' she answered. 'How are the dreams? Do you still have those?'

'Yes, but much less,' I said, 'and they've lost some of their intensity, it's like that power that they used to have has just gone. I don't really know why.'

'That's good,' Lorea jotted down a little note in her book.

'Yup. It is. But-'

Lorea tilted her head questioningly, 'but?'

'Well, it worries me that maybe the dreams are going because-' I found it hard to say, 'my memories of her are going. I don't want to forget her,' the thought was agonising, how could I forget my mum? I fought against it, against her becoming just a distant memory. 'I don't want to forget her. But the dreams, why are they going away?'

Lorea nodded, understanding and trying to reassure me. 'I don't think it's because you're forgetting your mum, I think you are just coming to terms with the situation, there's nothing you can do to change things. You have a lot going on in life. You're working and studying at college, which is fantastic. You are moving along in life, it doesn't mean that you're

157

forgetting her, Billie. Those dreams weren't good though remember, were they? They were traumatic, they didn't reflect your true relationship with your mum did they? Now you are living your life and not being upset by the dreams. Which is what your mum would want isn't it?'

'Yes, she would,' I knew that. Mum wouldn't want me to be traumatised for the rest of my life, she would have been happy to see me moving on. Moving on, but not leaving her behind. No. That was my worst fear, leaving her behind.

Lorea was happy that my psychotic symptoms had been gone for a good while and that I was doing well, managing my life and my loss. She would let Dr. Khali know and hopefully I would be able to come off the tablets and see how it went. I was pleased about that, but also a little nervous, I had come so far, I was scared of having a relapse and going backwards to that weird time when I was seventeen and eighteen, scared of hearing that crazy Mum's voice again, scared of having to go back into hospital. But I had to try, I didn't want to be on anti-psychotic medication all my life. I wanted to know how I would be without it, who my real self was now that I had grown up a little, achieved a little and become a little stronger.

Chapter 14

'Dad's got a date with Pat.'

I was coming to the end of the second year of my degree course at college. Laden down with a portfolio and my bag of art materials, Joni accosted me at the front door.

'Good for him,' I said, not for one moment believing Joni's appraisal of the situation.

'Yeah, you're not really listening,' she turned and sauntered back to the kitchen. 'There's a bottle of Charlie in his room, all wrapped up.'

'How do you know what it is, if it's all wrapped up?'

'I peeped inside the wrapping; he hadn't stuck it down very well.'

Teddy came up to me as I was dropping all my stuff in the hall.

'Hi darling,' I stroked his little scruffy white head and rubbed his ears.

159

Charlie, that strong, gets-up-your-nose-and-stays-there-for-a-week, type of perfume. Carly was wearing it, when I followed her around the vegetable beds of the walled garden that hot summer day in 1976. Even now, I could smell the air in her wake, see the warm bottle on the dashboard of the red sports car. I stood in the hall of our little house, remembering Northumberland on that sultry day, just before Mum disappeared. If only time had stopped still right then.

'*Yes, hello*, are you still with us?' Joni's sarcastic tone from the kitchen rudely interrupted my thoughts. '*So* what do you think?'

'Think about what?'

'*Dad. Date. Pat. Duh*. Wake up Billie, he can't go having dates. What about Mum?'

'Joni, for goodness sake. They're just friends I'm sure, But even if it is a date, *so what*? He can't be alone forever. Mum's gone; we know that. She's not coming back.'

Joni sat at the kitchen table dipping her finger in the peanut butter jar. Had I been too blunt? 'Sorry, I didn't mean to be short with you,' I sighed. 'Have you asked him if it's a date?'

'No, she hasn't,' Dads voice at the kitchen door. He walked in and kissed me on the cheek. 'She hasn't asked me, but I'll tell you both anyway. Here it is, I'll give it to you straight. Pat and I are more than friends, have been for a while actually.' He pulled out a chair and sat next to Joni. She was licking her finger and staring at him, ready for the next installment.

160

'I like her. I like her a lot. She's a good woman. But don't you ever ever think that I don't miss your mother every single day, because I do. I love her, I always will. You were right though Billie,' he looked to me and held out his hand, I took it and moved nearer. He continued, 'she's not coming back, it's been eight years now. She has died, I'm sure of that. She would never have let us suffer this long if she had been alive.' His eyes began to glisten. I put my arm around him. 'Dad, it's been long enough. You must have a life, and company and love again if you want to. It's none of our business anyway. Is it *Joni*?'

'No, it's none of our business,' she agreed.

'It *is* your business,' Dad corrected us. 'My business is your business; we are a family. I want you to know and I want you to be happy for me. That's all.'

'We are happy for you Dad,' I assured him and planted a kiss on his cheek, 'we are. *Aren't we Joni?*'

Joni nodded reluctantly. Dad pulled out a hankie from his pocket he gave his nose a good blow. 'Thanks girls, I knew you'd understand, you're good girls, a credit to your mother,' his eyes filled up again.

'Dad,' I said rubbing his arm, 'stop it, you're going to look a mess for Pat.'

He laughed, 'yes, yes you're right love. You see Pat makes me feel good again and that's why I like her. She makes me feel young, like I could be happy again, with another, you know-lady. Like nothing bad has happened. Or, at least, I can keep

161

the bad thing in its place. It has to be put away sometimes and kept there, in the past where it belongs. Otherwise we can't live, can't move on. You understand that Billie, don't you?'

I nodded and smiled through my tears. 'Yes Dad, I do understand. I really do. And I'm glad for you Dad, honestly I am.'

He gave his face a good wipe with a grey handkerchief, squeezed my arm, and went to get ready for his date.

'I just hoped Pat never wears *Charlie* in our house,' said Joni. 'It bloody stinks.'

I laughed and agreed with her. Then she added, 'it reminds me of Newell Hall for some reason, that scent.'

'I know, me too. Carly used to wear it.'

'Did she? Oh that's why then.' Joni leaned down, giving Teddy a lick of peanut butter off her finger. 'Strange times they were. Makes me feel a bit weird thinking about it. I feel as if there's a clue there somewhere, that we just haven't picked up on.'

'How do you mean, Joni?' I asked her, puzzled, although, I did have the same sort of feeling, but I wanted to know her perspective. We weren't children anymore. Perhaps something might come back to us that a child may not have thought twice about.

'Oh I don't know. Just that something happened to Mum, and we were there, maybe there could have been clues that we just didn't consciously notice. And if there were, they could still

162

be locked away in our subconscious, because we haven't had any revelations yet have we?'

'No, we haven't, I guess. Maybe you're right. But it's been so long now. You'd think if either of us had seen something linked to Mum's disappearance, a memory would have surfaced by now.'

It was 1984 and Dad was taking Pat to town for a meal and then to The Royal Court for a concert. We were left with tinned pie and chips for tea. 'My favourite,' said Joni as I struggled to open the hot tin without scarring myself for life. Aunty Jean didn't seem to come and cook for us so much anymore. I wondered if it was because she knew about Dad and Pat.

'Do you think she might be a bit jealous Joni?' I asked, 'not because she wants Dad for herself or anything, but just, you know, because, it's just been us and Aunty Jean for all these years hasn't it? I wonder if she's a bit, well, yeah, jealous, but only because, it changes things. Do you know what I mean?'

Joni speared a chip with her fork. 'Yes, I know what you mean. We've all been so close haven't we? We couldn't have coped without her.' She put the chip in her mouth. 'Actually, I feel a bit sorry for her. Maybe her nose is out of joint now.'

I pushed a bit of meat round my plate. 'Yes, that's it, we've been so close because of what happened to Mum. Because of our shared grief. But now, Dad's moving on. He's taken the next step, but Aunty Jean, she's still in the same place.'

'I feel so bad,' sighed Joni and she put down her cutlery, even though there was still food on her plate. 'What if Dad and Pat get married? Pat won't want Jean coming round making dinner for her husband, or us.'

'Okay Joni, I think you're jumping the gun a bit there,' I said. 'No one's said anything about marriage. They've just had a few dates that's all.'

'No, but it's the next step. It's the logical conclusion, especially for their generation. They're not going to live *over the brush*, or whatever it is they say at their age, you know. They'll get married rather than do that.'

I knew Joni was right and I felt uneasy about the whole thing. The Dad, Pat and Aunty Jean love-triangle and how would they fit together in the great scheme of things. I could not imagine and suddenly, it seemed the times they were a-changing. Life was moving on, soon I would be going into my final year at college and Joni would be starting her A' Levels. Who knew where life would take us or where I would be even a year from now.

'We have to take things as they come, Joni, Dad seems happy now, I'm glad about that.'

Joni took our dishes to the sink and started washing up. 'I suppose we could actually go and cook for *her* sometimes; Jean I mean. We're not kids anymore.'

And it struck me then, that she was right. All this time, Aunty Jean had been coming and looking after us, cooking for us, mopping up our mess and our tears. Perhaps it was time to

164

start looking after her now. 'You're absolutely right, Joni,' I said. 'We should go and cook for her, make her dinner sometimes, she'd like that, I bet.'

'Yeah, we could go and make her egg, beans and sausage on toast every Saturday night, see how she likes it,' Joni laughed.

After our conversation about Aunty Jean, Joni and I decided to take dinner to her house one Saturday evening after my shift at Bunnies. Joni had made a lemon drizzle cake and I had made a lasagne. We decided against the beans and sausage on toast option after remembering that we would have to eat it too.

'I think we should have told her we were coming,' I said to Joni.

'No,' she replied, 'I think we should give her a nice surprise.'

When we reached Aunty Jean's house it was all in darkness except for a dim light shining through the lounge curtains. I rang the bell, and it seemed an age until the front door opened. Aunty Jean stood in the dark hallway, looking a little dischevelled and flustered. 'Oh girls, what a surprise. I wasn't expecting you; I fell asleep on the sofa.'

'Sorry Aunty Jean, we should have let you know we were coming. We brought dinner,' I said.

'Yes, I mean no. Oh, I'm sorry girls, that's lovely of you, but I'm not really-' Jean started, but was interrupted by a male voice behind her. 'Who is it Jean love?' the voice said. It sounded familiar and then a face appeared behind Jean.

165

'Uncle Des?' I blurted out, unable to put two and two together for a moment. Then the penny dropped.

'Hello Billie, Joni,' Uncle Des nodded slowly and retreated back into the darkness.

'You'd better come in girls,' Aunty Jean said showing us into the kitchen. She disappeared for a few moments, and we heard low voices in the hall before the sound of the front door opening and closing as Uncle Des left.

'He didn't even say goodbye,' grinned Joni.

'Shh,' I said, shoving the lasagne into the oven.

Aunty Jean came back into the kitchen. 'I'm sorry you had to find out like that, girls,' she pulled a chair out, and sat down, re-styling her short greying hair with her fingers.

'Find out what?' asked Joni.

'Oh, you know Joni, don't act daft, Des and me.'

'Des and you? But he's married to Aunty Dawn isn't he?' Joni put into words what I was thinking.

'They split up love, a year ago now,' Aunty Jean told us.

We had never seen much of Des, Dawn and Rodney, only a few times over the years since Mum disappeared. Dad and his brother were never close, so we had not known that Des and Dawn had split up.

'Oh, I see,' I said. 'So how come you two got together?' I was completely baffled.

Aunty Jean was putting a pan of veg on the stove to go with the lasagne. 'We met in town about six months ago, I recognised him in the queue at C&A, he asked me if the

166

sleeves were too short on the jacket he was buying. We just seemed to hit it off, he made me laugh. And he realised he knew me, being your mum's sister. So we went for a coffee in town, then a meal and then-'

'Okay, okay, enough information thanks Aunty Jean,' Joni held up her hand.

'Oh no, nothing untoward,' Jean laughed. 'We went for drink at the Dog and Duck that was all, but we made a day of it that's for sure. We get along well, you know. We'd met before, mostly at your mum and dad's house parties over the years. But I'd never really known him very well.' Jean sat down at the table and poured us all some water from a jug.

And there we had been, worrying about Jean being lonely, now Dad was off dating Pat. I laughed inwardly, and she had been having a good time with Des all along.

'We were worried about you Aunty Jean,' I said, 'what with Dad and, oh, you know. Do you know?'

'Yes, love I know about Pat, and I'm pleased for your dad. Nina would be glad that he is happy, I'm sure she would.'

'We thought you weren't coming round because you might be upset about it.' Joni said, taking a sip of water.

'Upset? Oh no love. I'm not upset. Things have to move forwards, no point mooning about for the rest of our lives. You girls are moving on, we oldies have to do the same. I'm glad for your dad. But I'm sorry I haven't been around as much. I suppose I just wanted to give him some space. Give us all some space really.'

167

'We miss you coming round though Jean,' I said 'We really do. Today we thought we would bring your dinner round, seeing as you've cooked for us so much over the years.'

'I miss cooking for you all,' she said.

So we had our Saturday night dinner in Aunty Jean's kitchen for a change, and it wasn't bad at all. And afterwards, when we said goodbye, Jean said, 'I'll come on Tuesday and cook dinner for you all. No dates, tell your dad. It's a family night in, I've got sausages in the freezer and some beans I can bring, and we can watch something on telly afterwards, just relax together, like old times.'

Joni and I agreed this was a perfect idea. A sausage, beans and telly night, we could hardly wait.

I had continued working at Bunnies through my degree course. Nothing much had changed there, I'd had a meagre pay rise, other than that, things were still the same. Same regulars, same staff, same Graham. Things had been a little awkward between us for a while, but we were getting along great again now. After the Echo and the Bunnymen concert a couple of years ago, things developed between us, our friendship moved to another level, you might say. It was a great concert, and, high on the music, the atmosphere and the cheap lager, we had snogged. Yeah, it was a nice snog, and then we snogged again at various concerts and festivals, and then dated for almost a year. He was a good person, kind, thoughtful, we had a lot in common. But there was something missing, something I couldn't put my finger on, I just knew he wasn't right for me. Aunty Jean was disappointed because she liked Graham, but she understood my reasons when I ended the relationship.

When we returned to college in September I had thrown myself into my course and into my new and old friendships, first year whizzed by in a whirl of drawing, drinking and impromptu field trips far and wide in Greg's beat up van. We spent our days working away, printing and painting and life-drawing to the soundtrack of Lloyd Cole and the Commotions' *Rattlesnakes*.

At the start of second year, I met Geoff, a fine artist who looked like Jeff Bridges and smelt of paint and ale and smoke, an irresistible combination. We hit it off straight away, he made me laugh and I made him tuna mush. And about six months later, after a few TV dinners and bottles of Mateus Rosé in front of *Are You Being Served*, he was given the seal of approval from Dad, Aunty Jean and Joni and I knew I was onto a winner.

Chapter 15

Geoff didn't graduate with me because he dropped out of college after second year and started working in a call centre for a telecoms company. He loved art, but he wanted money too, he said. So he was still painting in his spare time and hoping to make it as an artist, but in the meantime at least he

169

had some cash. He was happy with that for now, and so was I, because he could afford to rent a nice little flat in the arty part of town and I spent a lot of my time there drinking beer and building up my portfolio.

Dad had taken the news of Aunty Jean and Des quite well. I think because he was with Pat by then, he wasn't too bothered what anyone else was getting up to. He and Des seemed to be getting along better now than they had when he was with Dawn. Dad told me they had always got along well as children, he wasn't sure what had gone wrong in later life, they had never argued or anything like that, just drifted apart. Mum and Dawn never particularly got on, maybe that was part of it.

On the day of my graduation we all went to town after the ceremony and had a slap-up meal at *L'Escargot*. Aunty Jean, Uncle Des, Dad, Pat, Joni, Geoff and me. It was quite a party; the red wine was flowing, and we all got quite tipsy.

'Cheers to you my clever daughter,' Dad held his glass of whisky aloft, 'our lovely artist, Billie, well done my love.' He planted a big wet kiss on my cheek. 'Thanks Dad,' I smiled, and he whispered in my ear, 'Mum would have been so proud of you.' I squeezed his arm and we both had a little tear in our eye. We all went back to our house after the meal, for coffee supposedly, but Dad opened the drinks cabinet and got out a good bottle of port and the soda fountain. I found some bags of crisps in the kitchen and Geoff put Joni's *Wham* LP on the record player. It was almost like one of those nights when

170

Mum and Dad would roll up the carpet for a party, but not quite. Not without Mum.

There was some dancing though, and a lot of raucous laughter at silly jokes. Around midnight, Des cornered me in the front room. He was the worse for wear, slurring and said to me, 'I'm worried about your Aunty Jean, love. I think she's ill, but she's not telling me anything much.'

'What?' I said, not hearing properly for the music, or at least hoping I hadn't heard properly. He leaned closer to my ear.

'I think she's ill. But she won't talk about it. See if you can get it out of her love, will you.'

'Well, yes, but why do you think that?'

Des took a swig of his port, 'she's been the doctor. She's got an appointment at the hospital next week for some test, but she won't tell me what it's for.'

I had been quite sloshed, but now I felt sober as a judge. *Aunty Jean, ill?* I thought. *Surely its nothing, but why won't she tell Des?*

'I will talk to her; I'll go and see her this week.' I assured him, 'don't worry, I'm sure it's nothing. If it was serious, she would have told you.'

He nodded, 'thanks Billie. Yes, she would have done that wouldn't she? Thanks love. You always were a good girl. Let me know what she says will you?'

'If she tells me, I will tell her she has to talk to you Des, it's not fair to leave you worrying.'

A couple of days later, I went to visit Aunty Jean. 'Des is worried about you Jean,' I said as we sat in her warm lounge, the sun shining in through the net curtains. 'He thinks you're ill and you're not telling him something. And now he's told me that, I'm worrying too.'

'Oh.' She stirred her tea, over and over, more than necessary.

'Jean? Please tell me if you're ill.'

'Billie,' she pressed her lips tightly together, then she said, 'yes, I might be, but I don't know for sure yet.'

I took a deep breath. 'What's wrong Jean?'

'Well, a little while ago I noticed a lump, here,' she indicated with her right hand to the outside of her left breast. I nodded slowly.

'I thought, oh it's nothing,' Jean continued. 'And then I carried on thinking it was nothing and did nothing. But it's got bigger, and sore. So they're going to take a sample of it next week.'

'Okay, good, good that they're going to check it out. I'm sure it's nothing Jean.' I smiled, she smiled. But deep down, we both knew that it could be something.

'I'll come with you if you like,' I offered. And I said, 'Jean, you must tell Des, he's worrying about you so much.'

Jean said that she would tell Des and that he would go with her to the hospital, and she thanked me for the offer.

'Hopefully it'll be nothing,' Dad said when, with Jean's permission, I told him about her health scare. 'She's indestructible is Jean, she'll be fine love. No point in worrying until we know exactly what's wrong.'

But he was worried, I could see it in his face. We all were, but we carried on with our day, I got ready to go to work at Bunnies and Joni was going out with her friend Gill. Dad and Pat decided they would take Teddy out for a walk round to Jean's. 'We'll perk her up,' said Pat, 'perhaps we'll bring her to Bunnies for lunch, eh Ron? What do you think?'

I liked Pat very much, she was a small woman with reddish brown hair, a permanent suntan and a friendly personality who was always up for an impulsive whist drive or a meal out. Dad seemed like he was actually living again after years in the doldrums. I thought Mum would have liked Pat, they might have been good friends- in a different life.

'If Jean is up to lunch at the cafe, then yes we can do that,' Dad agreed.

And they did come into Bunnies, Dad, Pat, Jean and Des, a nice double lunch date. There was a lot of laughter from their table, and they all seemed to eat well, full English all-day breakfasts all round. I was glad Jean had a good lunch because, I had noticed recently, she seemed to have lost a lot of weight.

That night Joni came into my room at midnight and sat on my bed. 'Do you think Aunty Jean will be ok?' she said. 'I don't know what I'd do if she- you know,' she sighed deeply, absently rubbing the hem of her nightie between two fingers, 'if anything happened to her.'

I sat up in bed, 'Joni, it's true what Dad said, there's no point in worrying, we don't know anything yet. It might be nothing.' I wished I could take my own advice, Jean was Mum's only sister, our closest link to Mum. I wasn't allowing myself to think too far ahead, to think the worst, but the thought of what might happen pushed its way in, insidiously, insistently, and it was an unbearable thought. I slept restlessly night after night, dreaming of Mum and Aunty Jean, horse-riding, dancing, cycling together and drawing Cleopatra eyes on each other in the 1950s. A strange confusion of the two best women in my life and their life histories all cobbled together like crazy paving. And me, falling through the cracks.

When I was young, I thought Mum was a film star, she had the best dresses, the best perfume and the best leading man. Poor Aunty Jean was ten years older than her, she worked for years at the tights factory on the outskirts of town while Mum gave up work to bring up Joni and me. I felt sorry for Aunty Jean with only memories of her tragic soldier boyfriend to sustain her. She never loved again as far as I knew, certainly she never married or had children. When I was a child I thought she had a sad life. But she didn't really, I realised later when Mum told me what a live-wire she had been in her youth. 'Oh yes Billie,' she had said, 'Jean was the life and soul of the party, even after Jim died, she got on with it, as she always does, pulled herself up by the bootlaces and carried on, in the wartime spirit. I was only seven at the time, but I

174

remember how it was. She was a lot of fun, your Aunty Jean, you might not think so, but she was.'

I was amazed at this revelation, and I couldn't quite believe it to be honest, I thought Mum was making it up because she felt sorry for Jean. But now that I'm older and wiser, I can understand that Mum would have no reason to make that up. There was no reason to feel sorry for Jean, she had overcome adversity and she was not dour or stern as Joni and I had once thought, but strong and resourceful and resilient. I liked to imagine Jean in her younger days, the Jean who booked a holiday for herself and Mum to go horse-riding on the South Downs. And I wished I could hear Mum tell me that oft heard story once more, because this time I wouldn't roll my eyes as I had done before, I would listen and smile and ask her questions, ask her to tell me again, just to hear her voice and the words falling from her ruby red lips.

The following week Des took Jean to the hospital for her tests, and then there was nothing to do but wait an anxious fortnight for the results. I was at loose end now, still working in Bunnies and wondering where my art qualification might take me.

'Are you in work tomorrow Bill?' asked Geoff one evening.

'Yes,' I replied, I was just putting a large tray of veg to roast in the oven. 'Maddie's increasing my hours this week now that I'm finished at college.

'Oh, ok,' he said, nodding, pressing his lips together, he looked thoughtful.

'Well, come on, penny for 'em,' I said sitting down opposite him at the kitchen table.

'Well, I'm just wondering about what you're going to do with your art now. There's not much going on here is there? In the art field I mean, for either of us.'

'No, I don't think so. It's all happening in London. That's where the magazines, and the publishers are. I've got a few business cards off people who came to the degree show.'

Geoff picked out an olive from the jar. 'That's what I thought. So, what about it then?'

'What about what?' My brows furrowed, though I think knew what he meant.

'London, do you think we need to move there?'

I took in a deep breath. I knew I had to think about it, but I just wasn't sure, it was such a big step to move all the way to the capital. But on the other hand, that's where the work was. I ran my fingers through my knotty hair. 'I don't know. I'm scared of moving to be honest. It means going so far away. I don't know, Geoff, I just don't know.'

'Well, we don't have to, it's up to you.' Geoff reached over and picked up a piece of my hair twirling it around his finger, 'just think about it, I will go with you, wherever you want to go. Or stay here. I'm easy.'

I laughed, 'okay, I'll think about it,' I said. And it felt good to know that he would come with me wherever I wanted to go. I looked at him with his Jeff Bridges eyes and his paint flecked hair and I felt happy despite the new worry which was steadily simmering at the back of my mind.

Jean and Des came round to Dad's house on Thursday afternoon, they had been to the hospital to see the consultant and find out the results of her tests. I knew this was the day, and all morning I had done nothing but worry.

'Well, its cancer, I think we all knew that.' Aunty Jean said, in her let's-not-make-a-fuss voice which we had heard so many times as kids. 'The doctor says I'll have an operation and then they'll find out if it's spread. They will start me on some sort of treatment probably then, when they know what they're dealing with.'

We were all sitting in the lounge, Des and Jean together on the sofa as if we were having a nice afternoon tea party, and how I wished we were gathered just for that reason. Aunty Jean smoothed down her skirt on her knee, as if to say: *That's it, that's all. I'll just have to get on with it.* But her face said, *I'm so scared.*

I got up and went over to her, I put my arms around her and hugged her. She seemed to melt into my shoulder for a moment, a moment of vulnerability in an otherwise stalwart woman. And then she patted my arm and sat up straight. 'Let's have some tea then and get on with things. I'll be fine. There's lots of treatments they can do nowadays, I intend to be around for a good while yet. So I don't want to see any moping on my account.' She stretched a hand over to Des and he held it tight.

177

That night I went to bed dreading the dreams I might have after the news that day, but in fact I dreamt of nothing, as far as I could remember anyway. I slept so deeply that I didn't hear the alarm when it went off at seven thirty the next morning. I was at home, not at Geoff's because of how upset we all were about Aunty Jean. Joni came in as she was leaving for school at half past eight.

'Hey, I thought you were at Bunnies today?' she said, waking me.

I jumped up and got ready in record time. I was half an hour late, but luckily Maddie wasn't in that morning.

'Hey Billie Holiday, nice to see you,' said Lenny as I walked in flustered and unkempt, throwing my coat in the kitchen and tying my apron on. 'Good morning Lenny,' how are you?' I said.

'All the better for seeing you love,' he answered.

'Where's Sam?' I asked, the two were rarely seen apart these days.

'Oh, he's gone down south to see his family, down to London. He's got a younger sister there and her husband he goes off to visit every now and then.'

'Ah I see, so you're on your own for a while, you must miss him.'

'Not when you're around Billie, I'm fine when I see you.'

I nodded and smiled half-heartedly; my mind wasn't on the job today really, not after the news about Jean. 'What are you having then Lenny?' I asked.

'The usual, Eggs Benedict please love. Are you alright Billie? You don't seem yourself today.' He looked at me kindly and with such an expression of concern that I burst into tears, standing there like an idiot, tears running down my face. He stood up and pulled out the other chair at his table. There was three other customers in the café, two women and a toddler. I was mortified, no one wants to see a crying waitress when you just came out for breakfast.

'Sit down, Billie. Come on, you tell me what's wrong,' he waved over to Graham. 'Bring Billie a coffee, lad, she's a bit upset.' He handed me a serviette to wipe my eyes.

'I'm alright, Lenny, honestly.'

'Sit,' he commanded. 'So I did. And I blurted out about Aunty Jean and her terrible diagnosis. I shouldn't have told him; it was Aunty Jean's private business, but he was so insistent and so sympathetic that I couldn't help it.

'Now you listen to me, Billie, your Aunty Jean has been around the block a few times. It's a shock, of course it is. But believe me by the time you get to our age, well, she's younger than me I know, but when you're getting on in life, you've seen a lot, you've seen friends and family die. And you know that when your time's up, it's up. And her time may well not be up. We don't know. But she will be alright. She has a lovely family supporting her and loving her. She'll get through, and so will you, it's not going to be easy, but you will. And you Billie, you'll be fine. You've weathered storms before, and you'll do it again. Mark my words.'

179

Graham came with Lenny's Eggs Benedict and my coffee, he put them down and gave me a sympathetic pat on the shoulder.

Lenny began tucking into his breakfast and said, 'now you drink that up and take it easy, you need to be kind to yourself, these are difficult times.'

'Thanks Lenny,' I said, dabbing my eyes with a paper napkin. And as I sipped my coffee, Katrina and the Waves came on the radio singing *Walking on Sunshine*.

Chapter 16

'Why did you argue that day Dad?' I had never asked that question before, I don't know why, it seemed the obvious one to ask. Start at the beginning. I was rehearsing in my room, in my head. I had wanted to ask that question off and on for years, but there had never been a *right* moment to actually let the words out of my mouth in front of Dad. Never wanting to put him on the spot or take him back to the nitty gritty of that awful day. Or perhaps I just wasn't ready.

But then, one unusually mild October afternoon, the *right* time seemed to arise, naturally. I was off that day from work and Dad was at home, at a raking up leaves from the lawn. I made us both a steaming mug of coffee with cream and a shot of whisky and took down the garden. We sat on the damp bench taking in the delicious autumnal aromas of smouldering leaves and coffee. Dad smiled at me and took a sip. 'Mmm, just what the doctor ordered. You're just like your mum, Billie, this is exactly what she would have done.'

'Dad,' I said, tentatively.

'Yes love,' he didn't look at me, he was admiring his lawn and the plants all neatly cut back, ready for their long winter sleep.

'Remember that day, Mum went missing?' Stupid question. Who could ever forget that day?

'Of course love,' his voice dropped and he was now looking downward, thoughtfully into the creamy depths of his coffee.

'Why did you argue?'

'We didn't really argue, love,' he took a deep inward breath and sighed. 'I'm sorry Bill, we should have had this

181

conversation long ago. I should have told you more. I don't know how much you knew already, but I suppose I was trying to protect you. Nina, Mum, I mean, had told me about six months before our holiday, that she'd been having a '*stupid fling*,' as she called it, with Frank. I don't think it was even an affair, just a few drunken fumbles. She wanted me to forgive her, wanted everything to be back the way it was. We did okay really on the holiday, till that night. The night before she went. I brought it up, I don't know why.' His eyes filled up with tears. 'If only I had forgiven her, if only I had put it in the past, the way that she was trying to. It was just a meaningless mistake. I loved her, but I wouldn't forgive her. If I had, she'd still be here. If only I hadn't been such a stupid, stubborn idiot.'

I put my free arm around his shoulder as he let the tears fall.

'You can't blame yourself Dad. You and Mum would have recovered from all that, what happened that day was no-one's fault, except, well, whoever else was involved. But it wasn't your fault, or mine or Joni's. All of us would have done things differently that day if we could have seen into the future. We all have our *if onlys* Dad. If only I had gone back into the cottage the day we left her there. I was so desperate to get to the beach, I didn't even say goodbye to her. It might have changed everything if I had gone back inside that day.'

Dad was shaking his head. 'No, Billie, it was me who stopped you. You wanted to go back in, you *asked* to, and I stopped

182

you. It is my biggest regret. I'm sorry, Billie, you were just a kid, I'm so sorry.'

And he hugged me tight and we soaked each other's jumpers in tears of regret and we both said lots of reassuring things but, no matter what we said, the *if onlys* would not leave us. Then I remembered Lorea's words, *'-she wouldn't have wanted her little girl to punish herself for the rest of her life would she? Do you think she might say: 'there's nothing to forgive?'* I knew, without doubt, it would hurt Mum if she knew we were living lives shrouded in *if onlys*.

'We need to know the truth, Dad. It is there, somewhere. Something happened to Mum and we need to know what it was. We need to find her and lay her to rest.'

'I know love, but it's a long time ago now, ten years. I can't see how we can find out unless something new comes to light.'

'Perhaps that thing needs dragging out into the light,' I said. Dad sighed deeply, 'I don't know how, Billie, I just don't know how.'

'By going back to the start,' I said. Back to the start. The holiday. The people there. The day she left.

'Oh Billie, that will be hard, painful, it can't do any good.'

'Dad, I have to try. The police stopped the investigation. There must be something, people don't disappear into thin air. We have to know what happened to Mum. I can't live the rest of my life never knowing.'

And first of all, I needed to speak to Carly.

183

Dad wasn't convinced it was a good idea but he would help me as much as he could and I was determined. All these years, wondering, waiting and hoping that Mum would be found and that all would come clear. That wasn't going to happen, I'd known that for a long time and now I was old enough to take some action. Even if it got me nowhere, at least I would know I had tried. So I went into a few travel agents and collected all the British travel brochures I could find. At home, Dad and I scoured each one, but we could not find Newell Hall in any of them. 'Maybe they don't do holidays at Newell Farm any more Dad,' I said.

'Perhaps not, I suppose the thing to do then, would be to go to the library and look in the local directories. So that's what we did. We made a day of it, taking a bus into town, exploring the art gallery and having lunch at the museum. And in the afternoon we went to the library, where, after much searching and a lot of help from the librarian, we found the number for Newell Farm, not in the phone directory, but in an old travel periodical from 1976.

When we got home at teatime, I decided there was no time like the present and nervously picked up the phone to ring the Newells. It was strange to hear Mr. Newell's voice again with its mildly upper-class accent concealing a faint north-eastern twang. 'Hello, Newell Hall, Robert Newell speaking.'

'Mr. Newell, hello. This is Billie Fisher; I don't know if you remember me? I stayed at Groom's Cottage ten years ago, in

1976. My mother went missing there.' There was a pause and a long intake of breath. I waited for Mr. Newell's response.

'Oh, my dear, of course I remember you. I have thought about your family many times over the years.' His voice sounded a bit shaky; I didn't know if it was because he was clearly older now and this was the voice of an old man, or because he was touched by emotion at the memories this call must evoke. And to be honest I felt a bit shaky too, I was connecting again to someone who belonged in the strange place and time that changed my whole life. We had a short exchange of niceties and then I said, 'I wondered if I could speak to Carly?'

'I'm sure you can dear,' Mr. Newell replied, 'but she doesn't live here anymore. She lives in Newcastle with her boyfriend and her little daughter.'

'She has a daughter?'

'Yes, Olivia, lovely child, only eighteen months old. If you give me your number, I will ask Carly to ring you if that is any help dear?'

I thanked Mr. Newell, and over the next few days I stayed home waiting. I didn't want to miss Carly's call. And then, on a Tuesday afternoon it came.

'I'm so glad you contacted me Billie,' her voice was the same, and I could see her again in that sunny field so many years ago, with her friendly smile and her blonde hair escaping from its ponytail. She continued, 'I've thought of ringing you again so many times. But, after the first year had passed, I didn't want to keep reminding you of that awful time. I thought

185

maybe I shouldn't call anymore, that I should leave you to get on with rebuilding your lives.'

When she said that, I felt very pleased for some reason, I think it was reassuring to know that she hadn't forgotten us.

'The thing is Carly; we haven't really been able to rebuild our lives because we still don't know what happened to Mum.'

I heard a gentle sigh down the line. 'I know, Billie, oh gosh, I'm sorry, it must be so hard.'

'I wondered if I could come and see you. If you don't mind that is?'

There was an almost imperceptible pause and then she said, 'yes of course you can. It would be lovely to meet up, I'd love to see you Billie.'

We organised a date and Carly gave me her address. When the conversation finished, I felt an overwhelming sense of achievement, as though I had done something amazing. And I suppose I had, because, at last, I was actually doing something to find answers to the mystery of what happened to my mother all those years ago. Carly was living in Newcastle so I booked a train and a B&B for two weeks' time as we had arranged.

Joan's operation was booked for two weeks' time, that was the soonest they could fit her in. 'It's not an emergency they say, but still, that's actually pretty quick,' she told us. 'And in the meantime, I don't want to do anything differently from the way we always have. I feel well, but I don't want to complete a bucket list or anything like that. I just want to spend time with my family doing ordinary things the same as we always do. Because that time is precious. More than we realise.'

I understood what she meant. Who wants to jump out of a plane when you could sit and talk with someone you love, have beans and sausage on toast with them, go for a walk in the countryside with them? One day that person's gone and the simplest things you did together become more precious than any bucket list. We were at home with Dad and Joni. Des and Pat weren't there, it was just us family, how it used to be just after Mum went. Dad and Joni were watching *Ask the Family* on telly in the front room while Aunty Jean and I were in the kitchen, me cooking up a throw-it-all-in-and-hope-for-the-best pasta dish, and Jean sitting at the table sipping a big glass of red wine.

'It smells good love,' she said. 'I do love a pasta dish.'

'Mmm, me too,' I agreed, 'I'm not sure about this one though, you might want to order something from the chippy.'

Jean laughed, 'oh no, it'll be lovely, I'm sure.'

I buttered some baguette and sprinkled it with garlic powder to put in the oven. And then, out of the blue, Jean said, 'I feel her you know,' I looked over to her. She was swirling the bowl of her glass gently round in her palm, warming the red liquid within it, her eyes fixed on me. 'Your Mum, Nina, I feel her, all around.' She sighed deeply.

I pulled a chair out and sat by her, pouring myself a glass of the Medoc. 'How do you mean?' I asked her.

187

'I don't know, I just feel she's here with me sometimes. Her presence or something. It's very reassuring in a way. Because, of course I will be going there too in the not-too-distant-future.'

'Oh Jean, don't.'

'I'm sorry love. I don't mean to upset you, but it's true, I will be going, hopefully not too soon. This feeling I have is only recent, I didn't feel like it before, All these years when we've wondered so many times what happened to her, she never came to me then, I don't know why. But now, it's as if she comes to me to guide me or ease my way.' Jean shook her head. 'Oh dear, the wine is loosening my tongue,' she smiled at me, and then rested her head on my shoulder. 'I shouldn't talk like this to you.'

'Of course you should, I want you to be able to talk about anything you like Aunty Jean, anything at all. What you say is lovely. Perhaps Mum is looking out for you, it's nice to think she's still around.'

But I wondered, if Mum was still around, wouldn't she be frustrated at not being able to talk to us? At being invisible? Wouldn't it be just too sad, watching from the outside while we are living our lives? Or maybe things look different from where she is, maybe she knows it will be the blink of an eye before we are together again, after all, eternity has no time-scale. I don't know, but I thought, *if it makes Aunty Jean feel better then its fine by me.*

Chapter 17

'Are you sure you'll be okay?' Geoff asked me as I packed a small overnight bag for my trip to Newcastle the next day. 'It's not too late to book another ticket. I can still come with you if you want me to.'

'No honestly, I'll be fine,' I told him. Geoff had offered to come when I first told him I was going to meet up with Carly. But for some reason, I felt that I wanted to do this by myself. I felt like I didn't want Geoff to become part of the *disappearing mother* trauma, I needed him separate, somewhere for me to escape to, somewhere safe where loss and pain were not in the equation. Of course, he knew all about Mum's disappearance and the aftermath, but he hadn't been involved in it all, he was a breath of fresh air in the whole sorry business. Geoff could see it all with objective eyes, and that was good for me.

'You take care then, Bill, okay? See you when you get back.' He kissed me goodbye as he dropped me off at the station. The train journey took four hours and I arrived in Newcastle at one o'clock on a busy Friday afternoon. I took a taxi straight across the city to the address that Carly had given me. The whole thing felt very surreal, like I was in a movie playing a part, an actress in a strange story, a bit of a thriller I suppose. I had a bit of a daydream about which actress I was. Annette

Bening I decided, she would play the part well. Yes, I could see her in my movie and, as I looked out the taxi window at the unfamiliar streets flashing by, I used my imaginary acting skills to convey an aura of trepidation, vulnerability and determination. I think I did it pretty well for a novice.

Carly opened the door, holding a young child who was clutching an eggy soldier. She looked the same, a little older but she had certainly maintained that *messy chic style* I had so envied at the age of twelve. Her hair was longer, still blonde, and as usual, pulled up into an untidy ponytail. She smiled, jigging the baby up and down on her hip. 'Hi Billie,' she said warmly, 'come on in, you must be tired after that journey.'

Carly led me through to the lounge where the floor was a sea of soft toys and ankle-breaking wooden bricks. She put Olivia down to play. 'She's so like you isn't she?' I said, offering the baby a strange looking giraffe toy as she toddled past. Babies weren't really my thing, but I had to admit, this one had something very endearing about her.

'Do you think so?' Some say she's like her dad. People see different things in children don't they?'

'Who's dad then?' The question came out typically badly thought-out. 'Oh sorry, that's none of my business.'

Carly laughed, 'no, no it's fine. He's someone I met at work. When we closed up the holiday cottages and dad retired from farming, I did a year of teacher training a took a job in Newcastle at the college. Matt's a teacher too. He's alright, yeah, not bad,' she smiled. 'Then Olivia came along quite

190

quickly.' Carly picked up the baby and offered her a cup of milk. Olivia guzzled it down, 'I'm just going to pop her down for a nap,' said Carly, 'I'll make some tea for us then, won't be a minute.'

While she was gone, I glanced around the room. It was cosy and comfortable with stripped wood floors and a scent of milk and laundry. Floaty grey curtains drifted on a breeze from the open window and I could hear the hum of the rush hour traffic outside. Carly came back minus Olivia and carrying a tea-tray. She poured the tea and sat on the sofa opposite me. On the wall behind her was an enlarged photo in a frame of herself riding Bay, there was a rosette on his bridle, it must have been taken at a gymkhana.

'I loved your horse,' I said.

She turned to glance at the picture, 'ah Bay, how I miss him. He was a real beauty.' She offered me the plate of biscuits. 'What are you doing now Billie?'

'I went to art college, but I'm still working at a café where I've worked for a few years now. I'm just deciding what to do with my degree. We might move to London, my boyfriend Geoff and me, but we're not sure yet.'

'Oh that's exciting, the world's your oyster. It must be lovely to work in art. You must be very creative.'

'Thank you,' I said, 'I hope I can work as an illustrator, that's what I really want to do.' I took a sip of tea and put my cup back down. 'But, well, we'll see. I never thought I'd ever get anywhere in life after- well you know.'

191

Carly nodded slowly, her eyes held mine steadily, 'I'm sure your mum would have been so proud of you.'

'I guess,' I said, looking down, thinking about my stint in the mental health unit.

'I'm sorry Billie, I didn't mean to upset you.'

'Oh no, I'm not upset, it's just that, well, I haven't done that great, not really. I went a bit, erm, off the rails for a while when I was about seventeen.'

'I'm sorry to hear that. But I'm not surprised Billie, you had a heck of a lot to deal with at such a young age.'

'The thing is, Carly, I need to know what happened to my mum. We all need to know.'

'Of course, I understand, I really do. I have racked my brains over the years to try and think what could possibly have happened to her. Even the police had no leads.'

'They were useless to be honest,' I said. 'As soon as they knew Mum had had an affair, they gave up on her. They thought she had just decided to take off, leave us. The case was closed very quickly because there was no evidence, no trace of her. But they didn't look hard enough. Something happened to her,' I stopped, because I could feel my emotions rising and I didn't want to embarrass myself or Carly by blubbing. I managed to hold myself together enough to add, 'It wasn't even a proper affair,' I laughed at myself, 'oh you know what I mean, it was just a stupid mistake. I know Mum would never have left us, she certainly didn't leave us for Frank, the man at Dad's work who she had the fling with. He

192

was still there when we got back. So why would she leave? I don't know. Oh God, sorry Carly, I'm really going on.'

'Don't apologise Billie, I can't begin to imagine how it must feel not knowing what happened to your mum,' Carly started picking up the empty teacups and added, 'do you know what? I'm sick of tea, how about I crack open a bottle of wine?'

I smiled, 'now you're talking, that sounds good.' So Carly went off to the kitchen and came back with a bottle of Pinot Grigio and two glasses big as goldfish bowls. She poured the wine, and I took a sip. The smooth, cold alcohol seeped through my veins. It felt good.

'Ooh thanks Carly, I needed that,' I said.

'Nothing like a nice Pinot to warm the cockles of your heart.'

'I've tried to think of anyone who might have known something about what happened to Mum,' I said. 'People I passed on the street or in a shop in Seahouses, someone who worked locally, or was just visiting. Over the years, I've tried to dig into my subconscious for any clue, any face who might have been hiding the truth. Anything.'

'The police spoke to Max you know.'

I raised my eyebrows and put my glass down on the table. 'Did they? I didn't know that.'

'Yes, and his wife. He told them he was working in the garden at Newell Hall that day, and then went home. His wife vouched for that.' Carly stood up and went over to the close the window. There was a chill in the air as the evening began to draw in. She pulled the curtains closed and sat back down.

193

'I was with him in the walled garden that day. To be honest, Billie, we had a huge argument.'

'Oh?' I didn't know quite knowing what to say. Of course, I knew, even at twelve years old, that Carly was having some kind of relationship with Max, but we had never spoken about it, of course, I was just a child.

'Yeah, he was no good to be honest, I was a pretty terrible judge of character at that time, but then, I was only twenty. We had an on-off relationship for a couple of years, then, when I came back from studying in Europe at the beginning of 1976 I found he had married a woman from Latvia, she was a migrant worker at the farm.' Carly laughed hollowly, 'well, I thought that was that, but he carried on coming to see me, you know. I was stupid to go along with it. But there was something about him. I couldn't seem to help myself.'

'He was quite good-looking, I noticed that even though I was only twelve.'

Carly laughed, 'yes he was, and he had some kind of charisma, he could charm the birds from the trees. But he wasn't a nice person- oh, he could be when it suited him, but only for his own ends. In reality though, he was-' she paused, looking for the word, 'volatile, yes, and manipulative. He was just out for himself, only interested in what he wanted, he didn't care about his wife or me.' Carly was swirling the last drop of wine in her glass before finishing it off. 'More?' she offered. I was lost in thought, taken back to that hot, oppressive summer. 'Oh sorry, yes, just a drop, thanks. So, what did you row about on the day Mum went missing?'

'Ah I finally found the strength to finish it once and for all,' Carly said, topping up our glasses. 'He wouldn't accept it, he tried to talk me out of it using all the charm he could muster. But I was determined to be strong. I wanted it over, and I wanted him to leave.'

'How did he take it?'

'He got angry, started yelling at me, showing his true colours. Max always *hated* not being able to get his own way. I remember him throwing down his tools that day and storming off. I heard his car screeching off down the drive. I wanted nothing more to do with him.' Carly smiled, 'it wasn't that easy though, he still worked for Dad, for the farm. So he came back a day or two later to finish off the walled garden. I avoided him like the plague so I didn't set foot in the garden again until it was finished.' She put down her glass on the table, and at this point there was a tiny murmur from Olivia's room. Carly laughed, 'oh poor Olivia, I've left her sleeping too long, she'll be awake all night.' She stood up to go and fetch the baby from her room.

'I'm sorry, that's my fault,' I said, 'I'm keeping you talking.'

'No, don't apologise,' Carly called back as she left the room, 'just one of those things.' She returned with the warm, rosy-cheeked baby wrapped in a soft blanket. Olivia stared at me, '*aggam*,' she said, or words to that effect, and pointed a baby finger at the weird giraffe thing on the floor.

195

'She loves that thing, God knows why,' Carly said as I picked up the toy and passed it to Olivia. 'Because even the ugliest things must have some redeeming qualities,' I said laughing.

Then I asked, 'what happened to Max? Do you know?'

Carly shook her head. 'He left with his wife, a few months later. I didn't see him much before he went, only when it wasn't possible to avoid him because of the work on the farm. But I know he was still there up until Christmas. I don't know where they went after that, didn't care to be honest.'

We said our goodbyes and agreed to stay in touch. When I was twelve years old, Carly seemed so much older than me. I admired her and wanted to be like her in my childish way. Now, I am twenty-two and she is thirty and the gap doesn't seem so great now that we are both adults. I returned to the B&B that evening, my head full of thoughts about Carly, Max and what on earth happened to Mum, it seemed I was no nearer knowing the truth about her disappearance.

And that night, I dreamed again, about water, a lagoon this time. The settings of my dreams seemed to get more and more exotic every time. A blue lagoon, like in the movie, it looked like Hawaii or Tahiti, somewhere like that. Huge, brightly coloured flowers and palms surrounded the lagoon and a waterfall poured into the beautiful, azure waters. Around the edge of the lagoon stood a line of beautiful women, all with long black hair and full, red lips, all smiling widely, wreaths of orange and white lilies around their necks. Their hips swaying gently in unison, and their voices singing out as one.

196

'*Would you like to spend Christmas on Christmas Island?*' I recognised the song we used to sing at our school Christmas shows. Why my subconscious was dragging it up now, in the middle of summer, I couldn't say. And then, there she was, at the top of the waterfall, Mum, in her orange and yellow floral bikini and a matching swimming cap. She waved and smiled to the singing islanders below whilst positioning herself at the edge of the waterfall ready to dive headfirst into the lagoon. I had that same sickening feeling again, watching her descend into the waters, I knew the horror that was coming and there was nothing I could do, but watch.

197

Aunty Jean had her operation, a mastectomy and samples taken from her lymph nodes and they took some scans of her other organs. Then a couple of weeks later, she was told that the cancer had spread to her lymph nodes and lungs.

'I don't want any treatment apart from pain relief,' she told us. 'I told the doctor there and then. I'm not stupid, there's no way they can get rid of this, my number's up and that's that.'

'Aunty Jean, please, they might be able to give you longer,' I tried to persuade her, but she was adamant.

'No, Billie love, it would just prolong the agony, for all of us. And anyway, they didn't offer treatment. They know it'd be a waste of time and energy. The doctors, they're not soft. They know what they're doing.'

There was no reasoning with her, I tried to tell her that sometimes the doctors *were* soft and that we would all support her if she wanted treatment, but she knew what she wanted, and what she didn't want. There was no changing her mind. Dad shook his head at me, trying to tell me to shut up and stop making it harder for her. So I did, I stopped. I realised I had to respect her decision.

Des took Jean home and for the rest of the evening, Dad, Joni and I sat in the lounge with the telly off, just quiet. We couldn't take it in. It was the worst news imaginable, since Mum. None of us really knew what to say. Joni burst out crying at one point. We were all upset of course, but my tears had run out over Mum I think, I was numb. Not that I didn't feel awful, I did, but I couldn't cry anymore, I didn't have the energy. And I think Dad was the same.

'She'll be well looked after,' Dad said. 'We'll all muck in, of course,' he lit a cigarette and went over to open the window, letting in the freezing night air. 'Joni, your Aunty Jean is a good woman, one of the best. Her time may be coming, but at last she will be with your mum again, so that's some comfort isn't it?'

Joni nodded, and smiled a red-blotched, teary smile. 'And Jim,' she said, 'she'll see her soldier, Jim again.'

'That's right love.' Dad agreed nodding.

I wasn't convinced, I liked the idea of being reunited with your dead loved ones, but I couldn't quite believe it. Aunty Jean would be about forty years older than Jim now, unless he'd aged in heaven or wherever he was, or unless, when she passed away, she went back in time to the age she was when she was going out with him. It was all way too complicated, but then I remembered that there's no time in eternity, so age probably wasn't an issue. I decided to try and convince myself of the possibility of reunions in the hereafter, because I could see that it would be a very comforting thought.

Over the coming weeks we all took turns visiting Jean, cooking, cleaning and keeping her company. Des was retired, but he wasn't always at Jean's house. We weren't sure where he went and didn't like to ask Jean for fear of upsetting her.

199

'He's a bloody wimp,' Dad said, 'always was. He can't take it when things get tough, turns tail and runs for the hills.'

'Oh Dad, it can't be easy for him,' Joni said, 'he's not long been with Jean, now he's losing her, it must be awful.'

'Of course it's awful, but you don't run off and leave someone in their hour of need.'

We had to let Dad have his little rant. I knew that he was very badly affected by Jean's prognosis. He felt, as I did, that we were losing our last precious link with Mum. The one person who knew her since the day she was born.

The phone call came out of the blue. I was at the flat that Geoff and I shared most of the time now. He was at work; I had been just about to leave for my shift at Bunnies. It was Dad on the phone, the police had called him. 'They've found a bag love. They think it's Mum's.' He couldn't say much more over the phone, too much emotion for his voice to cope with. I got in the car and drove round to the house. I felt numb, I couldn't think straight, all I could hear was Dad's voice. They've found a bag. Mum's bag, it could be Mum's bag. I couldn't take in the significance of this, we had waited so long for a break like this, now it seemed to have come I felt nothing.

I used my key and let myself in, Dad was sitting at the kitchen table, his head in his hands. I pulled a chair out, put my arm around his shoulder and kissed his head.

'I'd just got back from visiting Jean,' he said. 'The phone rang, and it was the police. A policewoman. She was very nice. She said the Newells had sold off the terraced farm cottages, you know, the ones across the road from where we used to stay? She said the new owners were renovating them and they found a bag, hidden behind bricks in an old bread oven. I'm not sure which cottage it was.' He gazed out the window at some kids on scooters in the street outside.

I was on Bay, circling the yard. I'd taken a wrong turn. We were walking past the row of terraces along the cobbles, it was so hot, so dusty, the sky clear and the air warm even so early in the morning. We came to the last cottage where Max was sitting on the steps, cigarette in his mouth, staring straight at me, unseeing. And there was the woman standing behind him in the shadow of the doorway, with sadness and anger in her eyes, and something else. Fear.

'There was a library card in the bag,' Dad continued, drawing me back to the present. 'Mum's name is on it. And her purse with the little bit of cash she had in it.' He started to cry and pulled out a handkerchief from his pocket. I stood and put both my arms around him, tears pricking my eyes too.

'We'll deal with this, Dad. Whatever's happened we'll deal with it together.' We'd been through the worst already. We had lived through every possibility over the years grieved and hoped and grieved again, imagined the worst but hoped for the best. Now perhaps, at long long last, resolution was coming.

We drove up to Newcastle, Dad, Joni and I to see the bag. To grasp the one clue, the one last link to Mum. The bag and the items from it, were each in their own clear, plastic wallets.

Detective Inspector Charlotte James carefully lifted each item out of its wallet with gloved hands and laid them out on a clean white cloth like precious gifts. And that is what they were, precious gifts given up at last by the bricks and mortar of that cottage at Newell Farm. The yellow handbag itself, looked scuffed and scraped on the outside and the gold clasp broken. For a second, I saw Mum's hand, smooth and slim with red polished nails, snapping that once shining clasp shut, as she had done so many times. The inside was empty and lined with gold coloured fabric.

Then the purse, brown leather and empty of its few coins and its library ticket. So many times she had handed me a few pennies from that purse for the pick 'n' mix counter at Woolworths. *'Here love, go and get yourself some sweets while I look at the records.'* And the library ticket, a dog eared, oft used, brown cardboard library ticket, for a long-forgotten book, on the slip inside it, her name: *Edith Nina Fisher.* I caught my breath.

Dad was strong, he didn't break down. Just nodded and said 'yes' as each item was shown to us. Until it was all done. Then the police took us to a small room, a family room. Light and airy, painted in calm colours, greens and blues to comfort grieving and traumatised people. We sat down on the soft green sofas.

'Finding Edith's bag is a major step in our investigation. The case into her disappearance has been reopened,' DI James said.

'*Nina*, her name was Nina,' Dad said.

'Of course, my apologies,' the DI James replied.

'So, that man, Max lived in that cottage didn't he? Where is he now? He must know about the bag,' I said.

Dad and Joni looked at me, puzzled. I felt like I'd been withholding information. But I had never really contemplated the possibility that Max had anything to do with Mum's disappearance, I knew he was around at that time, but I had no reason to link him with her. Until now.

DI James took a deep intake of breath, 'we are attempting to trace him, but it seems he returned to Latvia with his wife some years ago. Yes, it does, on the surface appear that he may know something about Nina's disappearance.'

'Of course he must know. Why else would her bag be in his cottage?' I could feel my blood rising.

'We must take things one step at a time. My officers are reviewing the case and taking into account all the new evidence,' DI James began.

'And what about Mum?' I interrupted. 'Where is she? She can't be far from the cottage; he must have hidden her the same way as he hid her bag.'

'We are investigating all the possibilities at this present time.' Charlotte James seemed to be stuck in police-handbook mode, under the section- *How to Respond to Awkward Questions from Disgruntled Relatives.* I'm sure she was a nice person, young, bright and successful. No doubt she had risen quickly up the ranks despite her sex because of her determination and

203

talent. But she needed to adapt her responses. I'd heard them all on *The Bill*.

I was trying hard to control my emotions. After all the years of waiting, hoping, wondering, now it seemed we could be close to finding out what happened to Mum and I wanted nothing to jeopardise that. 'Well, I hope you do a better job than the original investigation did,' I said. 'They gave up on her. Did you know that? You would have still been at school then, but yes, they gave up on her, thought she'd had an affair and wasn't worth investigating.'

Joni put her hand on my arm, 'Billie,' she said calmly.

'No, Joni,' I wasn't in the mood for arm-touching or hand-holding, I was too angry now, trying to keep control. 'They need to find her this time. They *have* to find her.' I looked at DI James who was nodding slowly, her striking green eyes fixed on me. 'We will find her,' she said, 'we will Billie, this time. I promise you.' She promised. *Is she allowed to do that?* I wondered. *What if she can't deliver? Then what?*

Dad stood, and offered his hand to DI James, 'thank you, we'll go now, thank you for your time.'

'Not at all,' the DI shook Dad's hand. 'We will be in touch.'

The police requested that we did not talk to anyone else associated with the case until they had completed their investigations. They would be speaking to Carly and Mr. Newell. Now everyone was a suspect. So, although we were in Newcastle, I didn't see or speak to Carly, and it felt wrong. Carly was a friend; I knew she had nothing to do with Mum's disappearance. But there was no way I was going to jeopardise the investigation.

That night I dreamt. There was no idyllic preamble this time, no sunny Hawaiian island, no bright flowers, or lapping waves on a sandy beach. This time Mum was in a tank. A huge, sealed tank, full of dark green water. It was in a room not much larger than the tank itself, and lined floor to ceiling with huge grey slabs of stone. I could see no door, no escape. I could only just see Mum's face inside the tank as she came near to the glass, the rest of her body flailed around in the water and Joni's stone pendant floated up around her neck like a hangman's noose. She was mouthing something to me. I stepped nearer trying to see what she was saying. Her eyes were desperate, pleading through the glass, bubbles floating up from her red lips. *Help me Billie, please, I'm here, can you see me? Please get me out.*

'Strange things dreams, they tell you things you thought you didn't know. But actually you *did* know all along,' the old man at the library had said so long ago. I woke with his words on my mind. Did I have some knowledge that might lead me to Mum? Some memory stored away that I needed to unlock from the deepest recesses of my mind, and if so, how?

A couple of days after we returned from Newcastle Aunty Jean was taken into the hospice. The pain was getting too much, she needed more specialised palliative care now. I couldn't bear the thought of her dying, but like King Canute trying to hold back the tide, I could do nothing to prevent the inevitable. We visited every day. I told her all the things I needed to, like how I loved her, that I appreciated all that she'd done for us over the years. All the things I never said because she would have rolled her eyes and told me to get on with my dinner. She still rolled her eyes but she was smiling, and I know she was pleased to hear all those things.

'I love you too, silly Billie,' she said. 'Never was much good at emoting, but I do love you, and Joni, and your Dad.'

Even though it's a pretty miserable stage to have to go into hospice, the staff there were incredibly positive and they kept Jean's spirits up. They always talked and acted like every last drop of life is worth investing in, worth planning for, which of course, it is.

One Monday teatime, DI Charlotte James rang me. 'I spoke to your dad, but he wanted me to call you with information,' she said. 'He thought you could relay information more clearly in person to him. Is that alright with you?'

'Of course,' I replied, 'thank you.'

'Oh Billie, not a problem, is it alright to call you Billie?'

I agreed to that. And she asked me to call her Charlotte. It seemed fair but very familiar, much easier though, that's for sure.

'Okay,' I said. 'Do you have more information?'

'We have conducted forensic tests on your mother's bag. There were grazes across the surface of the bag, and fine grains of grit embedded in those areas. The grit is consistent with grit underlying the road surface near to Newell Farm. We

206

think the bag was somehow dragged along the road there with some force, but we do not know how. It does suggest a road traffic accident perhaps, but we are keeping an open mind at this point.'

Geoff was in the kitchen with me, listening, tea-towel in hand, watching my face turn from animated to slow-mo to pause and stop. I put down the phone calmly. I went into auto-pilot, not daring to really examine the implications of this news, it was too much, just too much to take in all at once.

'They think it may have been a road traffic accident. Maybe, not absolutely sure. The bag looks like it had been dragged along the lane with force, right there near the farm.' I grabbed my coat off the door. 'I'm going to see Dad and Joni.'

'Want me to come too?' Geoff called after me. But I was out the door. 'No, it's okay,' I called back, 'I'll see you later.'

  'The hospice just rang, Jean's taken a turn for the worse,' Dad said as he opened the door. 'I was just about to go and see her.'

'Okay,' I said. 'I'll come with you.'

'Were you coming to see me for anything in particular?'

'Er, no, it can wait. Come on let's go.'

Chapter 18

Just as it seemed that perhaps we were coming closer to finding Mum it looked as though we were closer to losing Jean. My heart was heavy seeing her lying there, her skin waxy and pale, her breathing laboured. The sweet, cloying scent of death drifted in the air.

'How are you love?' she said, her voice barely a whisper.

'Never mind me, I'm fine, what about you? I hope you're planning to rally round soon,' I smiled the smile of a person ready to descend into a black hole of despair.

Jean sighed; her eyes filled with tears. 'I hoped we would find Nina before I go. I want to know what happened to her, where she is. That's all.'

'I think we're getting nearer. Please hold on Jean. *Aunty* Jean, please, we need you. I need you.' I wanted to cry out, wail, yell at the doctors, shake them by their white lapels. Instead we were just quietly losing her, and I knew I must be strong, as strong as she had always been for us. I stayed with Dad and Joni, we needed to be together at a time like this, all together for Aunty Jean, so that we could go to her day or night.

In my dream I was twelve years old again and back in the bedroom at Newell Hall, the one where we stayed just after

Mum disappeared. I woke in that unfamiliar room with an awful feeling of emptiness and fear and worry. It felt like the whole world had changed in the blink of an eye. And then I heard those noises again, coming from the garden. I got up and went over to look out realising that my window looked out over the walled garden. And there was Max, digging and breaking stones for the new pond. He was covered in mud and a huge mound of earth had formed at the side of the deep hole which would be the pond.

As I looked out, Max raised his head as if he knew he was being watched. I stepped back from the window, embarrassed to be caught watching him, but too late, he had seen me. In that second, I saw his mud-streaked face with a cigarette hanging from his mouth and his eyes fixed on me like a rattle snake hypnotising its prey. And I *was* hypnotised I stopped where I was, still visible to him. He leaned on his spade and took the cigarette out of his mouth. And his sullen expression changed suddenly into a grin, a leering, sneering grin. I shrunk back further behind the curtain and stayed there, too frightened to move for what seemed like ages.

The noises carried on, the sound of scraping and the banging and cracking of hammer on stone, so I knew Max was still working. Eventually I found the courage to move myself. I washed and dressed quickly and went down to find Dad and Joni playing cards.

Then I woke. Stunned, I lay there staring at the ceiling with my heart beating out of my chest, hardly knowing where I was for a moment, so vivid was the dream of that morning so long ago. He was in the garden, Max, digging the pond, with his heavy spade going deeper and deeper, scraping the earth out of the hole and lining it with huge, grey slabs of stone.

Joni came into my room, and she sat on my bed. 'The pond.' She said it calmly, as if I already knew, as if she was just reminding me. And I did already know.

'The pond at Newell Hall.'

Charlotte James seemed unconvinced about the pond. I didn't tell her about the dreams or anything like that because I knew I would sound ridiculous. But I told her that both Joni and I had good reason to believe that Mum may have been buried under the pond.

'It would take a lot of manpower to dig up the pond, especially, if, like you say, it is lined with stone flags. I will have to look at all the evidence and discuss it with the Chief Superintendent.'

'But there isn't really a lot of evidence is there?' I said. 'I can only tell you why I feel she may have been buried under the pond.' So I told her about Max and how both Joni and I had seen him digging the pond and breaking flags to line it just two days after Mum went missing. And I told her how he looked up at me and grinned in that ominous way.

'I understand it was a very strange and difficult time for you Billie, but you are giving me the memories of a twelve-year-old child from ten years ago. I cannot order a team to dig up the grounds of Newell Hall based on that evidence. The Chief Superintendent may sanction it. We will see.'

'Well please remember to tell the Chief Superintendent that the man digging the pond, two days after my mother's disappearance also had her bag hidden in his house- or have you forgotten that?' I said to her.

Charlotte sounded irritated and I was worried she was going to switch to *Police Handbook* mode, but as she continued, her voice seemed to soften a little. 'No, I have not forgotten that and I will make sure he has all the facts in front of him. We must go the right way about this. I promised you Billie, we will find your mother and I will do my very best to keep to my promise.'

'Okay, good. Thanks. And what about Max? Is anyone going to go and find him in Latvia?'

'Yes, I was coming to that actually,' Charlotte said. 'We have traced him and two officers are going out to Latvia this week to interview him.' She paused and then added, 'he's already in prison, so he's going nowhere for now.'

Edith Nina Fisher neé Baker was my mother. She wore floral dresses, orange and pink, and her blonde curls bounced off her shoulders as she walked. She kissed my cheek with the rubiest red lips you've ever seen. She told me once that she wanted to be like the movie stars she had seen at the Woolton Picture House. At the time I had no idea why because I thought she was more beautiful than any Hollywood star of the silver screen.

'She was never made to be a housewife,' Dad said.

'She was good at what she did though Dad,' I countered. 'She was loving and generous, a great mum.'

'Yes love she was, yes, a great mother, she loved you girls more than anything in the world, she wanted the best for you.'

She read picture books to Joni and me, *The Hare and the Tortoise* was her favourite. 'The hare thinks he's the bees knees' she said to us, 'he thinks he's the fastest, the cleverest. But the tortoise doesn't rush or worry, he goes patiently and slowly and he gets there in the end, safe and sound.' She brushed our hair and plaited it, made us dresses on her Singer sewing machine, took us to school and brought us home again. And she held my hands as we swayed in the kitchen to *That Ole Devil Called Love.*

I wanted nothing more than you three, she said to me, *you are all I ever needed, I promise you that Billie.*

And then one day, one hot summer's day, a red car driving too fast, blaring music, windows down, smashed into her, sending her high into the air and skidding along the road with her yellow bag and her library ticket inside it. And she lay there moaning in the empty country road, the only witness, a blackbird singing in a tree high above.

And he wrapped her in a blue beach towel with a picture of a yellow yacht on it and threw her broken body into the boot of the red car and slammed the lid shut. Then he picked up her yellow bag with her library ticket and her purse inside and shoved it under the passenger seat. He wasn't really thinking straight. This was an unusual situation, but he would work out what to do. He hadn't really meant to hit her, but it didn't matter. He had been arguing with Carly. Carly had made him angry, so it was her fault this had happened. But this woman, the one in the road, was no doubt just as stupid. A typical woman just like his wife and Carly. Selfish, vain and disloyal. No one would miss her. What's to miss? So he left her in the boot for a couple of days until he worked out what to do.

- - -

We didn't tell Aunty Jean about the circumstances of Mum's death. About how Max had killed her, that she might have survived if he had called an ambulance, how she was still alive when he put her in the boot of his red car. We didn't tell her that he had buried her two days later under the pond at Newell Hall which he had then lined with stone. We told her that Mum had died outright in an accident and that she had been buried in a copse of trees on a hill overlooking the sea.

'I saw Nina you know, in a dream,' Aunty Jean said to me just a few days before she died. 'She said she was waiting for me and-' her voice was weak and faltering, she was on high doses of morphine, but I knew she wanted to tell me something.

'Your mum told me to tell you that she's alright, and she will see you again one day. *Be patient, like the tortoise* she said. What does that mean Billie? Do you know?'

213

I live life each day as it comes now, and I feel Mum is okay. Not knowing what happened to her haunted us for so many years and then, when we found out exactly what did happen, it tormented us all over again. And then one day, Dad said to me: 'Her ordeal is over, terrible as it was, for her it finished years ago. It's us who relive it again and again, torturing ourselves. And in the end there comes a time for letting go. That's what she'd want, Billie love. She'd want us to let her go.'

Geoff and I moved to London the following year, we rented a garden flat on Charlotte Street and life was good. I'm expecting a baby now, a girl, yes, and she's feisty, I feel her kicking and rolling in the warm depths, raring to get out and sock it to us. And we will call her Nina Jean after the two best women I've ever known.

Chapter 19

I am walking across the lawn toward the walled garden. A warm breeze lifts my hair and the wet grass bathes my naked feet. I can hear a bird, a robin I think, singing in a yellow rose bush whose heavy scented petals have already begun to fall. I push open the ancient and rotting wooden door and step into the walled garden. Clematis and nasturtiums rise high along the trellises, and the woody aromas of sage and rosemary fill the summer air. I walk along the redbrick path; my feet numb to the grit and sharp stones beneath them. I know where I am going. I can see the house rising beyond the walls, and the unseeing eye of the window where once I stood looking out onto this view.

And there is the pond, surrounded by its grey stone walls. No fountain in the middle, no reeds or irises or duckweed to soften the edges, no dragonflies or water boatmen to play on the surface. It is just a pond full of darkness. I reach the stone wall and lean over. I see my reflection looking back from the still sheen of the blue-black waters. I have big eyes like Mum and full red lips, and my hair is blonde and curled like hers. Just then, behind me, the sun comes out and suddenly the water is lit up with the reflected blue and white of the sky. I can see clearly now as her beautiful face floats up breaking the surface of the water and she lies there quietly, like Ophelia peacefully sleeping. Her eyes are closed and her perfect red lips unmoving.

And there, against the smoothest white skin of her neck, lies a gold thread and a duck-egg blue stone flecked with bright copper.

- - -

Printed in Great Britain
by Amazon